COULD TH[E] LEGEND B[E SO] DEADLY?

There was a legend once. A Legend that said somewhere in the depths of space was a planet of wealth and power beyond imagination. It was also a planet of danger and mystery. The name of this planet was Heartworld. It was the planet where mankind had sprung from, the planet from which the original colonists of Earth had had left in search of a new star system—a new home. But now, eons later, no one on Earth believed this pretty fable. The Heartworld was a pleasant fairy tale meant for children and the nostalgic at heart. But then one dark evening a drunken spaceman named Joe Chattan, stumbled into the life of a stranger covered with mysterious tattoos. This stranger proved to be the gateway to discovering the truth behind the myth—the myth of a forgotten planet laden with so much power that no one man could be trusted with its control.

Join science fiction icon Edmond Hamilton as he takes you on a mad race across the star ways to a deadly planet where the legend is reborn…

FOR A COMPLETE SECOND NOVEL, TURN TO PAGE 93

CAST OF CHARACTERS

JOE CHATTAN

This spaceman was looking to relax after a long day, but seeing a stranger being mugged led him into a mad dash across space.

SHOBA RUK

He was part of a traveling show on a carny ship. To most he was a harmless idiot; to Chattan he was a tattooed mystery to be solved.

BETTA BREWER

Smart and pretty, she wasn't exactly your typical carny daughter, but she knew how to take care of herself when fists started to fly.

DOC BREWER

As the kindly owner of an interplanetary carny show, he was known to have big heart for all his performers.

LAURENCE HARVEY

He held a lofty position as one of the directors of the C.R C. But he was a man who would stop at nothing to obtain the ultimate power.

FARAH

A slimy merchant from the Thieves Star. He was all about money and power, but teaming up with Joe was not in his plans.

BARBOUR

A dirty cop from the Earth Planetary Police and one of Laurence Harvey's bodyguards. He would do anything for his boss.

.

THE TATTOOED MAN

By
EDMOND HAMILTON

ARMCHAIR FICTION
PO Box 4369, Medford, Oregon 97504

*For more information about Armchair Books and products, visit our
website at…*

www.armchairfiction.com

Or email us at…

armchairfiction@yahoo.com

CHAPTER ONE

THE GIRL WITH the golden eyes and warm green skin was becoming too friendly. Joe Chattan shook his head at her and laughed. He was a little drunk, but not too drunk to remember that he had to be back aboard the *Phoebus* by midnight. He dropped two coins together into the girl's bodice, and patted her cheek, and left her, steering a difficult course between the crowded tables.

Outside the low doorway, the steaming air of the world called Rigel Two did very little to revive him. One big bright moon was overhead, and another was in the act of setting. The shadows ran confused between them, and the coils of mist were like silver floss, blowing gently through the streets.

Feeling as though his own head was beautifully stuffed with mist and moonshine, Chattan smiled and set out toward the starport.

The streets straggled every which way. This quarter near the port was crowded and squalid, like similar quarters all over the lanes of galactic trade. The houses were flat-roofed, with high narrow fronts, and they were full of smells and cries, laughter and muffled voices, shaded lights. There was nothing to tell a drunken spaceman which street he was on. Chattan got lost.

"Oh, well," he said to himself cheerfully, "there's no problem. All I have to do is stop and listen."

He stopped, with the bright mist curling around him. He listened.

In a few minutes he heard the distant, deep-toned thunder-clap of a ship in take-off. A streak of fire mounted slowly up the sky. Chattan turned himself to face it and began to walk again. The streets twined and twisted, narrowing, widening, crossing open courts, clambering up and

down steps. The moon was playing a game of its own, shifting stealthily around the sky so you couldn't get a bearing on it. Pretty soon, in a court between four quiet walls, Chattan stopped again.

He listened.

He did not hear any ship. But he heard another sound.

The confused, fierce, furtive sound of secret violence.

Chattan's face tightened and his eyes became foggily alert. There was a narrow alley opening off one corner of the square, and the sound seemed to come from there. He went quietly over to it. He was not in search of trouble. He was merely curious, and in the back of his mind hovered the thought that a fellow spaceman might be in need of help...a not unusual thing in neighborhoods like this.

He looked into the alley.

In the chequered moonlight, he could make out the forms of four men. One of them was half crouched with his back against the wall, moaning like a hurt beast and striking out with his hands at two of the other men, who pounded and

battered at him. The fourth man stood by and watched, his tall body bent forward in an attitude of intense excitement.

"Now," he said. "Now!"

He spoke in good Earth English, and Chattan frowned.

One of the attackers moved in swiftly and struck down, hard. The man with his back against the wall whimpered and slid to the ground.

Instantly the two had him pinioned, his arms behind his back and his face strained up into the moonlight. It was a dark face. It looked black, but it might have been any of a dozen colors by day. There was a network of silvery markings on it, scars possibly, or some form of tattooing. It was a good face, with a fine high brow. It was also, incongruously, the face of an idiot. The eyes stared, full of fear but without understanding. The mouth opened and closed and panted, but no word came out, even of protest.

The tall Earthman who had spoken before said, "Hold him." He bent closer to the pinioned man. "Lugach," he said. "Lugach?"

The dark man whined and tried to break away.

7

The Earthman spoke rapidly, almost savagely, in a language Chattan did not know.

The dark man made no response, except to whimper.

In what amounted to an outburst of insane fury, the Earthman struck the dark man several times across the face, continuing to speak in that unfamiliar tongue.

Chattan stepped forward. He had only one good reason. He was mad. It seemed a hell of a way to treat a helpless halfwit.

The halfwit suddenly voiced a mighty cry and sent sprawling the two men who held him. It was as though those blows in the face had shocked some deep-buried center of pride and human rage. He sprang forward at the Earthman.

"Good for you," said Chattan. He charged at the two men who were getting up off the ground and preparing to attack the dark man from the back.

After that nothing was very clear to Chattan. The moonlight was full of fists and a bobbing in and out of angry faces. Curiously, there were no weapons used. But the men were good fighters. They knew all there was to know about alley brawls. Chattan found himself on the broad of his back, and when he looked around he saw that the halfwit had the Earthman down, and that the other two men were beating and kicking him away, Chattan got up, shook his head, and charged again.

This time he got hold of the Earthman. He had a very brief but fairly clear glimpse of a thin intense face, corroded to the soul with one of those austere passions that amount to monomania, and that leave no room for any softer consideration of mercy or common fairness. Chattan's drunken perceptiveness saw this, and saw also that this man was no ordinary thief or footpad, but something much more dangerous.

He understood suddenly that he had stepped into something evil and complex, something that was none of his business.

And it was too late, entirely too late.

ALL AT ONCE the Earthman had a weapon. Chattan saw it. He grappled for it, his hands around the Earthman's wiry wrist. The Earthman came in close against Chattan, his eyes glazed and shiny like two big beads, his mouth twisted. The weapon made a quiet hissing. Smoke sprang from Chattan's uniform coat. He gave a deep shuddering groan and fell down into the dust.

He had a dream there. He was all alone, floating in a silent brilliance that reeled and swam, and he was in very great pain. After a while the moon came down to look at him, and the closer it got the darker it got, until it was all black except for a seaming of silver. Then even the dream was gone.

When he woke again the pain was still there, but dulled and far off. The queer brilliance was gone, swallowed up in a flat grayness of painted metal against which a single light-tube burned. There was something familiar about that metallic ceiling, and that particular type of fixture. Chattan frowned, and then he remembered, and a vague alarm that had been plucking at him subsided. He was looking at the ceiling of a ship's cabin. It was all right, then. He had made it back to the *Phoebus*, after all.

He lay feeling peaceful and relaxed, listening to the heavy throbbing whine of generators in the deep vitals of the ship. The *Phoebus* was already in overdrive, out between the stars. He must have been unconscious a long time, he thought. He could not remember anything about take-off, or acceleration run, or shift.

The generators sounded funny, somehow, but he refused to let it worry him.

The cabin door opened and a girl came in. She looked at Chattan and smiled and said, "You're awake. That's good. How do you feel?"

She came and bent over the bunk, and Chattan stared at her. There were no girls aboard the *Phoebus*.

"What are you doing here?" he asked.

"Taking care of you."

"Yes, but *here*. Aboard ship."

She looked at him, puzzled. "I live here."

She was a small girl, one of these pert, peppery types, with brown hair cut short, and extremely blue eyes. She moved lightly, as though her slim body was made all of spring steel. She looked competent. *Tough* was the word that came to Chattan's mind, but it wasn't quite the right one, because her eyes were compassionate and good-humored.

He said weakly, "Since when?"

"All my born days," she answered wryly, and then asked. "Where do you think you are?"

A small wedge of panic entered him and widened rapidly. He looked past the girl, around the cabin. It was not his. The sound of the generators became even stranger in his ears.

He said, "The *Phoebus?*"

She shook her head. "This is the *Merry Andrew*. It's a carny ship. Travelling show, you understand? It belongs to my father, Doc Brewer. I'm Betta." She began to peel the sheet back, exposing his chest. "What's your name? You didn't have any papers on you when Lugach brought you in, nothing to tell…"

"Lugach!" Suddenly Chattan remembered the fight in the alley, the idiot, the Earthman with the wild fanatic face. He looked down at himself. His left side was bandaged. He remembered the Earthman's weapon, and he remembered falling…

He began to sweat. "What happened?" he said. "I mean, after…"

"After you were hurt? Lugach came back to the ship, all beaten and bruised. He was carrying you. He can't talk, but we've got so we understand him pretty well. We gathered that men had attacked him, and you had saved him, and been hurt doing it. We thought at first you were dead. Dad wanted to leave you behind, but Lugach roared, and of course he's our main attraction, so Dad has to keep him happy. So we brought you along!"

"Well," said Chattan. "Thanks."

She grinned. "I put in for Lugach. It seemed the least we could do." She was checking the dressings, very skillfully.

"Didn't you even try to find out what ship was missing a mate?" he said angrily. "I suppose you realize I've lost my berth and probably my ticket… I'll have one blazer of a time explaining…"

She answered curtly, "You're alive, aren't you? Be thankful for that." She pulled the sheet back up. "We didn't have any time to ask around. Dad just bundled up the show and took off. We can't afford any more trouble than we've got, mister, and when we found out that Lugach had been attacked again, we…"

"Again?" said Chattan, startled.

"This is the second time. Before, it was on Mars. Two men came around to the show, and they asked my father a lot of questions about it, and about Lugach, where he came from and so on, and Dad was feeling good as usual, and he fed them a fine line of taffy, all lies. That night the same two men tried to kidnap Lugach. Rival show, I guess. We couldn't think of any other reason."

"Was there a third man? A tall Earthman, kind of fanatic looking, with a thin face?"

She shook her head slowly. "I didn't see anybody like that."

"He's the one who shot me. And he seemed to know Lugach. Personally, I mean. He called his name, and he spoke to him in some language I don't know. He seemed to be *questioning* him, and then he went into a wild rage when he didn't get any answer. Started beating him…" Chattan paused, and then asked, "Who is this Lugach, anyway?"

"Just a harmless idiot," said Betta, with a note of fondness in her voice. "Dad bought him a couple of years ago, off a tramp skipper who'd picked him up at Algol One… you know, that unfederated system they call Thieves' Star. How he got *there*, is a puzzle. But dad figured he'd be a draw as a curiosity. Wait, I think there're some posters here."

She began to rummage in a locker. "Don't believe a word of what it says, though. Dad made it all up out of his own head, on account of the way Lugach is tattooed. All we really know about the poor soul is his name, and we wouldn't know that if it wasn't tattooed right on his own hands. Yes, here they are."

She turned around, holding a gaudy poster. On it was a picture of Lugach, full length, in a striking pose, wearing nothing but a fancy kind of short kilt. His skin showed here as a deep garnet color, almost black, and it was patterned all over with the weird silvery markings. His face, in the picture, was lofty and remote.

The legend, splashed in huge letters across the poster, said LUGACH… KING OF THE FIRST-BORN! SEE THE MAN FROM THE HEARTWORLD, CRADLE OF HUMANITY… WIN A THOUSAND CREDITS IF YOU CAN READ THE MYSTERIOUS RUNES OF POWER WRITTEN ON HIS SKIN BY THE HANDS OF THE ANCIENTS!

In more restrained type was added, "Standing offer from Scientific and Research Foundations across the Galaxy. You may be the one to solve the age-old mystery of Man's Origin!"

"There isn't any offer, of course," said Betta, "any more than there's really a Heartworld. It's all hogwash but you'd be surprised how many people fall for it! Dad's safe, though...the tattooing doesn't mean a darn thing."

"I wonder," said Chattan, with a sudden odd feeling of fear.

"What do you mean?" asked Betta.

"It must mean something to that Earthman," said Chattan. "He was willing to kill me to get it."

CHAPTER TWO

THE *MERRY ANDREW* droned steadily through space—sub-space or hyper-space, whichever you preferred to call it... heading toward Sirius. And Joe Chattan put in the dull hours of flight and convalescence thinking.

Thinking hard. Because somewhere down in his subconscious mind was the conviction that he was not through with this curious dark struggle, whatever it meant.

He had seen the face of the lean Earthman, and the Earthman had shot him, and left him for dead in the alley. He would be dead now if it had not been for Lugach. Presumably the idiot had run out of reach of his assailants at that point, and then had come back for Chattan when they left...probably hurriedly, since the row must have been heard in the surrounding houses.

But the Earthman had paused long enough to take Chattan's wallet, containing all his papers and all his cash. Why? Obviously to make it seem that some ordinary lurking thief had killed him.

And why had he been shot at all? Three active men could more or less easily have subdued one somewhat drunken spaceman. Or they could simply have gone away from him. They had not used any weapons on Lugach. Why then on him?

Obviously, because he had seen the Earthman's face, and he had seen what the Earthman had been up to, and he could tell about it.

The Earthman, Chattan thought, might be someone relatively easy to identify, someone of importance. And if that was so, it was something mighty damned powerful that would drive him to the acts he had committed.

Something connected with Lugach.

Doc Brewer didn't think so. Doc Brewer was tall, good-looking and affable, the sort of man you like on sight and wouldn't trust with a counterfeit nickel. He sat with Chattan in the main cabin drinking decorously and quarreling with Betta over their show's projected itinerary, which he was drawing up. And he said, "Some rival outfit is trying to get him, and that's all. If he had his wits they'd hire him away, but he hasn't, and so they have to use other methods."

"Do you think," asked Chattan, "that he's valuable enough for someone to follow you all the way from Mars to Rigel Two?"

He looked over at the idiot, who was sitting as he always sat, his hands palm-down upon his knees, perfectly still, his dark, silver-scarred face intense and withdrawn, bent over his hands as though some great secret was written on them that he must solve.

Brewer grunted impatiently, "Who said they were the same men? Lugach pulls 'em in everywhere, and there are hungry angleshooters on every planet." He grabbed suddenly for the chart sheet. "Now what are you crossing out Betelgeuse for?" he demanded crossly of his daughter. "We did fine there the last trip…"

"So fine," said Betta sarcastically, "that we left owing nine hundred and sixty-seven credits for fuel and repairs to the *Merry Andrew,* and if we go within ten parsecs of that system you are in trouble." She took the sheet back and drew an emphatic line through Betelgeuse.

"Well," said Brewer grudgingly, "all right. I'd forgotten that."

Chattan was still studying Lugach. The man fascinated him. In spite of his mental lack, there was a nobility about him, the dim echo of something lost.

"He wasn't born an idiot," Chattan said.

"Who knows?" said Brewer.

"Look at his face," said Chattan. "He's no youngster. I'd say he's older than you are by ten years. Those years left marks on his face, and I'll bet you anything you like they weren't lived by an idiot. Look at him now. He always seems to be trying to remember."

"Yes," said Betta. "I know, poor fellow. And he does have a fine head. I suppose it could have been a birth injury that made him that way, even so."

"Or something that happened to him later," Chattan said slowly. "A shock…torture, an ordeal of some kind…those marks on him might be a clue. I've never seen anything like them before."

"That's what makes him valuable," Brewer said. "Nobody else has, either."

"And you haven't any idea what world he came from?"

"Whatever it was," said Brewer, laughing, "it wasn't the Heartworld. But don't tell, or I'll be out of business."

No, Chattan thought, it wasn't the Heartworld. Only people who liked to believe in wonders and the truthfulness of myth still clung to that ancient galactic legend. He himself had believed in it as a child. It was a fine stirring legend and it was a pity it wasn't true, but that was one of the penalties of growing up, that you had to let so many of the fine things go.

IN THE BEGINNING, the legend said, there was one world and one race of men. There were a lot of different descriptions of this world and these men, according to who was retelling the story, but the important fact was the uniqueness of the human race and its appearance on this single world of all the swarming planets of the galaxy.

These men were very wise, and they could do anything. They built great ships that flew among the stars, and everywhere they went they planted colonies, conquering one wild system after another for the use and service of mankind. And, said the legend, that was the Golden Age of galactic man, because the colonists grew and became a mighty empire that spanned the stars, and all men were brothers, united by a single heritage and a single loyalty to the Heartworld from which they came.

But time passed, the legend said, and the people of the colonies lost their singleness of identity, adapting to the different conditions of their different worlds, so that after a while there were many colors among them, and many statures, and many different tongues. And they forgot that they were brothers, and made war on each other, and the great golden Empire fell and there were ages of chaos, when the people of the colonies sank back into barbarism and the starships rusted away because no one knew how to fly them. And even the Heartworld was lost, except for the nostalgic legend that ran through the folklore of countless scattered stars.

Even of the star called Sol, which if you believed the legend must have been so far on the frontiers of the Empire that it would have been among those colonies first forgotten.

Even on Earth, on Sol Three, there were folklore traces of the old story. And that legend did furnish a beautifully simple answer to the problem that had astonished the first Earthly outrovers to other stars...namely, the prevalence of humanoid races on every world within habitable limits.

A little too beautiful and simple an answer. For the Empire and the Heartworld were only dreams. People who believed in them and tried to prove they had existed were in precisely the same position as those Earthmen who had once insisted on the reality of Atlantis.

So Lugach did not come from the Heartworld. But he might have come from any of a score or so known planets, where conditions had produced that particular shade of skin among at least part of their inhabitants. Which was very little help.

"But the Earthman knew," said Chattan.

Brewer looked at him.

"He spoke to him," Chattan said. "In a particular language. Not Universal, but a particular language."

"Doesn't prove a thing," said Brewer. "Lugach didn't answer, did he? All right. Your Earthman could have been just trying out a language on the chance that it might be the right one." He shook his head. "I don't think Lugach's got a language. Even his name is tattooed on him in Universal script. I think somebody did that so he wouldn't have to learn a new name to answer to every time he shifted around."

"A funny place to put it," said Chattan, "on the backs of his hands, and right way up for him to see. And it's funny how he sits there by the hour, staring at them."

"What else has he got to look at?" said Brewer, laughing. "You've got too much imagination, Joe. You belong in the carny business."

In a curiously sharp tone, Betta said, "Oh, no, Joe's strictly a spacehopper."

"I was," said Chattan. "Lord knows what I am now. That'll be up to Spaceman's Hall, when we land."

"Well," said Brewer, "we can all swear to what happened. You won't have any trouble."

Chattan said, "I hope not," rather gloomily.

BETTA SCRATCHED two more names off the itinerary sheet, and Brewer howled. They began to wrangle again. Chattan looked at Lugach, at the silvery spiderweb of lines on his dark skin. They were like tattooing, and yet not like it. They were like the scars of old, thin wounds, and yet not like them. They were like writing, like intricate design, like… well, like almost anything you wanted to make of them. His mind reverted to the Heartworld legend.

Lugach sat and looked at his hands.

Chattan sighed. Old tales. Dreams and moonshine. Nothing.

And yet the Earthman had tried twice to capture Lugach. He probably would try again.

Well, thought Chattan, there's a simple answer to that. The Earthman is crazy. It showed in his face, all right. Man with a bee in his bonnet. Whatever he thinks or believes about Lugach, it doesn't have to be so.

Forget it.

It was easy to forget things. He was still weak as a kitten, and all he had to do was close his eyes. The voices of Betta Brewer and her father receded into a comfortable distance, blending themselves with the background noises of the *Merry Andrew*, the throb of the generators, small iron creakings, whines, and clatterings from the ship itself.

The few animals belonging to the show lived in the central hold, and their somnolent gruntings and occasional statements of resentment or rage came muffled through the ventilator shafts. The human members rattled around in the cabin decks, twenty-two adults in all, including cook and helper, animal man and helper, roustabouts, and performers, but not including the men who actually piloted and served the ship and who bunked on the bridge-deck.

The performers, Chattan had noticed, all seemed to be very young ones on their way up, or worn-out ones on their way down, or middle-aged ones who had accepted the fact that they were not going anywhere. They had transformed the cabin decks into a species of bustling tenement, complete with children of all ages and colors, and the corridors resounded with voices and the thumping of feet...and several different kinds of music.

It probably wasn't a bad life, Chattan thought drowsily, if you had no ambition and didn't care if you were broke. But he wished he were back on the *Phoebus,* he wished he were in his old bunk right now, sleeping...

Someone screamed, a knife-edged, nerve-slashing shriek of sheer panic.

Chattan sat bolt upright, so sharply that he pulled his side and almost fainted from the pain. Betta had sprung up, too, and her face was pale. Doc Brewer was swearing looking in mingled anger and apprehension toward the door to the main corridor.

"What," said Chattan shakily, "the hell was that?"

"I'm afraid it's Preek," said Betta.

"Preek?" Chattan had met Preek, a plump butter-colored little Mintakan who did a mind-reading act, and was always as cheerful and indolent as a well-fed baby. He got up painfully and started toward the door. "We'd better see what's happened to him. Maybe one of the animals..."

"No," said Betta. "It isn't as nice and simple as that. I wish it were. Preek's a genuine sensitive."

"Most of his people are," said Chattan, still prodded by the terror in that scream. "I don't see what that's got to do with it." He continued toward the door.

Feet came running down the corridor, small heavy feet moving fast. Preek burst in through the door. His golden skin was greyish and his curly brown hair clung to his head, damp with sweat. His eyes, normally sleepy and rather vague, were as wide and dark and shining as the eyes of a frightened deer.

He stopped just inside the door, looking from one to the other, half seeing, half blind.

"A shadow passed over the ship," he said. "Evil and hate went by us, *there!*" His arm described an arc, indicating the passage of something which was now ahead of the *Merry Andrew*. Then he shivered, and his voice sank to a childish whimper. "I can smell death," he said. "Betta, I'm afraid."

He went to her and she put her arms around him. "There, there," she said, but her face was anxious.

Without warning, the idiot rose from his corner and stood up. His eyes burned with a great light. He clenched his fists and cried out in a loud voice.

"Lugach," he said. *"Lugach!"*

"Good God," said Doc Brewer, astonished, "he said his name!"

CHAPTER THREE

THE CARNIVAL PITCH on Sirius Five was an acre or so of flat dusty ground adjacent to a corner of the starport. The city beyond was indistinguishable from the city on Rigel Two. The same lofty buildings rose in the distance, glittering in the overpowering blaze of the mighty sun, monuments of interstellar trade erected at this contact point. Between the lofty buildings and the port the same kind of squalid slum spread over the land, a less lovely monument to interstellar relations.

Chattan stood blinking in the relentless glare, watching the roustabouts haul out the light plastic shelters, brilliantly colored and considerably patched. By a lower hatch, the animal man was superintending the unloading of various cages. Chattan said, "It seems peaceful enough."

"I hope it stays that way," said Betta. "But Preek just isn't ever wrong."

Doc Brewer grunted. "I'm going to get rid of that little curse. I'm sick and tired of having my sleep ruined by his crepe-hanging. A man gets enough trouble without having to worry about it ahead of time."

"When are you going to fire him?" asked Betta.

"Well," said Doc. "Sometime. Soon. When I can find an act to replace him." He went off to oversee the setting-up, and Betta grinned.

"The heck he will," she said. "Dad never fires anybody, and if they leave him he's blue for days." She shook her head. "Poor Dad. He's no doggone good, and I know it, but what are you going to do?"

She turned to look at Chattan. "I suppose you'll be going back to your ship."

"I suppose so."

"Then I suppose this is goodbye."

"Oh, no," he said quickly. "I'll be back." He reached out and caught her hand. "Listen, Betta. I want to thank you for all you did…"

She drew her hand away. "It was no more than I'd have done for anybody that was hurt."

"No," said Chattan. "I suppose not. But thanks anyway. And…" He stepped forward and put his arms around her and kissed her, hard. "That's no more than I'd do for anyone who saved my life."

"Then," she said, in an odd, quiet voice, "you better do the same for Lugach." She withdrew from him, and smiled, and said, "Good luck, Joe, let us know how you come out."

Rather stiffly, Chattan said, "I will. Well, so long."

He turned and walked away from the *Merry Andrew*. Lugach was inside, as a safety measure, and locked up to prevent his wandering or being lured away. After his dramatic statement of his name...the first word Doc or Betta had ever heard him speak...he had lapsed back into his brooding silence.

Chattan stamped angrily through the dry blazing heat and the dry white dust. He did not understand why he should be angry. It just seemed that Betta might have been a little more...well, friendly.

At the edge of the pitch he met Preek, who was helping to put up the light collapsible boundary fence. In a small outfit like Doc Brewer's everybody had to help with the work of setting up, and tearing down, and there were two others with him. Shemsi the physical superman from one of the heavy worlds of Betelgeuse, and Lute the Capellan, a small furry individual from arboreal habitat who did incredible things on the high trapeze. They all stopped what they were doing, and Preek looked at Chattan, and then he turned and looked toward the city. And he said, "The sun does not shine on you, Joe, and when I turn toward the city I see a red shimmering of danger."

Shemsi said, "Preek knows. You better not go." And Lute nodded solemnly, his eyes shining like emeralds in the silky pale hair that covered his face.

"But I have to," Chattan said, half annoyed at Preek, half upset in spite of himself. The Mintakans were, as Betta said, genuine sensitives, and there was nothing supernatural about an esper picking up strong vibrations of malice, from the minds of other men.

It was perfectly possible that the thin-faced Earthman had got here ahead of them in a faster ship. A check with port authority on Rigel Two would give him the *Merry Andrew's* destination, and if he was still after Lugach he would certainly come to Sirius Five.

It was also perfectly possible that he knew by now that Joe Chattan's body had not been found, and that therefore Joe Chattan was very likely not dead. He might deduce that Chattan was also aboard the *Merry Andrew,* and he might decide to do something about that, too.

Still Chattan had to go into the city. If he didn't report himself now to Spaceman's Hall and get himself straightened out, he would never get another berth on a decent ship, let alone a master's ticket.

So he nodded to Preek and the others and said, "Thanks anyway for the warning," and walked on into the hot crowded streets of the city.

MONEY WAS MADE in the high serene towers, and great decisions were carried out that affected whole sectors of the galaxy, but it was here in the swarming starport quarter that life was lived, noisily, actively, and with no little violence.

Men and women of every color in the human spectrum, dressed in every conceivable costume, moved like a sort of sticky kaleidoscope along the streets and around the market squares and in and out of the bars, tenements and gambling houses. They were the poor of the galaxy, the deserving poor looking for a better break, the undeserving getting rich on dishonesty and vice, the merely incompetent settling like the blown dust into the puddle where chance had put them. Mingled with them, but not of them, were the men from the starships, living it up to last them until the next world fall.

It was all familiar to Chattan. He had, been here before, and he had been in a hundred other places just like it. It should not have been disturbing, or menacing.

It was. The glare of Sirius blinded him in the open street, but under the walls and in the covered ways the shadows were black and fun of whispers and unseen movement. It was hot, and he sweated, but the sweat turned cold on his skin. The babel of voices, raucous cries, music, colors, smells, the swirling pushing movement of crowds, all confused him, and he felt that under cover of these distracting things he was being followed, watched, threatened.

He cursed Preek. He stiffened his back and walked steadily, neither slow nor fast. Once or twice he yielded to temptation and looked behind him, but he could not see anything in particular. About halfway to the Hall his new-healed wound began to ache and a great weakness came over him. I'm not able to do it today, he thought. I'll go back to the ship and rest until tomorrow. Then he thought angrily, Bull! I'm just looking for an excuse to duck, and I'm damned if I will. He walked on, his jaw set grimly.

Nothing happened.

Spaceman's Hall was a typically shabby building crowded in between a house of joy and a poverty stricken importing firm. Everywhere there was a starport there was a Hall, adjunct of the Interstellar Spacemen's Federation, where a member in good standing could apply for a job or iron out a grievance, or try and explain why his ship had taken off without him.

Chattan went inside, into a narrow longitudinal hall with several doors. The doors had signs over them. About midway down was one that said SECTION 6, and under it "M. Quard". Section 6 of the Federation's Standard Contract covered violations of the type Chattan was concerned with. He opened the door and went in.

Quard was a Sirian, a large dark man behind a cluttered desk. There were two other men with him. They looked up as Chattan entered, and they smiled. They were both Earthmen. Chattan knew them. He had seen them once before, by moonlight, in an alley on Rigel Five.

Chattan stopped. The two Earthmen got up, and Quard said to them, "Is this the man?"

One of the Earthmen looked at a photograph attached to some papers he held in his hand. He looked at Chattan, and said, "Yes."

Quard said, "Chattan? These men have a warrant for your arrest."

Chattan took a step forward. "Arrest!" he said. "That's good, coming from them. Look, those are my papers they stole from me, after their pal shot me and left me for dead." He leaned over Quard's desk. "How can they arrest anybody? They're not cops, they're..."

"But they are," said Quard, cutting him short. "I've already checked into that, very carefully."

Chattan looked from him to the Earthmen. "I don't believe it," he said, and measured, desperately, the distance between himself and the door.

ONE OF THE MEN had now moved and placed himself between Chattan and the exit. The other shrugged and produced credentials.

"I'm Barbour," he said, "and my partner is VanFleet, Earth Planetary Police, Detached Unit, on special duty with Interstellar Research, empowered to make arrests under Interstellar Code regulations covering the rights of nationals. Here's the warrant."

Chattan read it. It authorized the arrest of Joseph Henry Chattan, a national of Sol Three, for assault with intent to commit great bodily harm upon the person of Laurence

Emmett Harvey, also a national of Sol Three. Details of the assault followed, sworn to by Laurence Emmett Harvey, and by officers Barbour and VanFleet, who had accompanied Harvey as his bodyguard. The details were all there, except one.

"You forgot," said Chattan, feeling the sweat run down his back, "the most important thing of all. You forgot Lugach."

Barbour said, in a tone of mild puzzlement, "Lugach? What's that?"

Chattan turned again to Quard. "There're lying," he said desperately. "This Harvey thought he'd killed me, but he didn't quite, so now he's taking this way to shut me up. He and these two so-called officers were beating up one man in an alley, a poor devil of an idiot who couldn't defend himself..."

"An idiot?" said Quard, frowning. "What are you talking about?"

"A freak from a little carnival. They'd lured him away, and these two beat him down and held him while the other man, Harvey, tried to force him to talk."

Barbour laughed. "Well," he said, "that's one for the books."

VanFleet laughed too. "Mr. Harvey collects a lot of things, but carnival freaks just aren't on the list. I'm afraid you were seeing things that night, Chattan. You were blind drunk. Crazy drunk, I should say."

Chattan said to Quard, "I have witnesses."

"Present them in court," said VanFleet. He laughed again. "But you're going to have a hard time making any judge believe that Laurence Harvey goes around beating up carnival freaks."

Now, through the reactions of fear and frustration that were clouding Chattan's mind, that name... Laurence Harvey... linked itself with the name of Interstellar Research, and rushed suddenly into center focus. Interstellar Research, biggest of the giant commercialized research corporations that bulked so large in a galaxy dominated by technics. Chattan swore under his breath, feeling the imponderable weight of millions of dollars and the power they can buy descending on his head.

"So that's who it was," he said. "Laurence Harvey. One of the three directors of Interstellar. No wonder he didn't want to be recognized."

Barbour and VanFleet closed in. "Come along, Chattan."

Chattan sprang.

He drove his fist hard Into Barbour's face, feeling the flesh splay out like soft rubber under his knuckles. Barbour fell aside, and Chattan caromed into VanFleet. VanFleet grappled with him, and they danced round and round in a sort of wild waltz, Chattan striving to free his arms and hit VanFleet, VanFleet trying to hang on and at the same time to hit Chattan. Quard stood up behind the desk and shouted at them, punching buttons.

Chattan pulled back and landed a solid kick in VanFleet's gut. VanFleet let go of him and bent double, his mouth open. Chattan bolted for the door, but Barbour was on his feet again now, with blood dribbling out of his nose and a grin of pure fury on his face. He had pulled a gun out from under his tunic.

"Stand still," he said to Chattan, "or I'll cut you in two.' "

Chattan hesitated. There were voices and movement in the hall now, men running. VanFleet was still struggling for breath. Chattan looked at Barbour's gun.

"You going to kill me here," he asked, "in front of witnesses? Mr. Harvey won't like that."

"Just stand still," said Barbour. He began to walk forward.

The door burst open. Men came in, asking what the trouble was. Chattan took the last chance he was going to have. He flung himself straight at the group bunched up in the doorway.

There were eight, maybe nine men there. Even so, he almost made it, through them and into the hall beyond. Almost. Not quite. They caught him and held him, pinning his arms, and a second later he felt the hard little snout of a gun rammed into his spine, and Barbour's voice said, "I told you to stand still."

He stood still. There was nothing else to do.

CHAPTER FOUR

TIME HAD PASSED. Chattan knew that because the lopsided patch of sunlight from the high window had moved all the way across the opposite wall and was now disappearing altogether. The room was getting dusky, so that the figures of the three men looked shadowy and enormous.

Harvey, VanFleet, and Barbour. Barbour, VanFleet, and Harvey. Shuffle and reshuffle. Play it hard, play it soft. Play it anyway, and it still added up two angry men and a hungry one. Chattan shook his head and blinked, and tried to see clearly the face of Laurence Harvey.

It was Harvey's turn again, and he was playing it soft.

"You didn't understand that night," he said, "and I don't blame you. It looked bad, what we were doing. Of course it did. And I made things worse, I admit. I shouldn't have shot you. But my nerves aren't good, Chattan, not at any time. I panicked. I thank God I didn't kill you, and I'll make it up to you any way I can...money, a job, anything you want. Now is that fair?"

Chattan said, "Just let me go. That's all I want."

"Later," said Harvey. "This isn't settled yet. It's important that you understand..."

"I understand," said Chattan. He spoke with some difficulty because his lips were cut and swollen. "You're crazy. You've got money enough to go ahead and be crazy, and nobody cares. You can buy guys like Barbour and Van-Fleet, by the dozen if you want 'em. What do they care if you're crazy?"

"But I can't buy you. Is that it?" asked Harvey, and smiled. "All right, I'll accept that. It isn't true that every man has his price, no matter what they say. Then I'll have to get at you another way."

He leaned over Chattan in the gathering dusk, his pale thin face alert and quivering, his eyes bright with that look of austere and ruthless passion that Chattan remembered so clearly. Instinctively Chattan pulled back, but the chair stopped him. He was tied to it, so there was nothing he could do but look up at Harvey, and listen.

"I'm a very rich man, Chattan, and the resources of Interstellar Research are practically unlimited. Between them I've been able to do a great deal of studying all over the galaxy. The more I did the more I came to believe that a legend like the story of the Heartworld couldn't have risen out of nothing. Other people have thought that, but they didn't have the money to carry through. I did."

He moved away, walking back and forth, his feet making a dry clacking sound on the floor tiles. The shadows grew thicker in the corners of the room, and the sounds of the city were far off beyond the window. VanFleet and Barbour waited, resting. Their turn would come again.

Harvey said; "You think I'm crazy. I won't argue that. You think I've become a fanatic on this thing, and I won't argue that, either. You laugh out loud when I tell you that the man you call Lugach knows where the Heartworld is, and I don't blame you for laughing. But you may find it less laughable when I tell you that his name is *not* Lugach, that I know him, know who he is, studied under him and with him on his own world, and sent him out eight years ago on an expedition to prove my theory about the location of the Heartworld."

He swung around, thrusting his face close to Chattan's again, speaking now with a cold furious violence that was shocking to a man tied down and unable to fight.

"The Heartworld had many names in legend. Trace them back, and as the forms of the legend get older the names get older. The oldest ones are Lludoc, Lukah, Hludag. Does that suggest anything to you?"

Chattan closed his eyes to shut out that face so close to his own. The eyes were hypnotic, compelling belief by the sheer force of their own belief.

"It suggests to me that you're willing to accept anything to prove your theory," Chattan said. "Maybe you sent an expedition out, maybe you didn't. I don't know, and I don't care. Maybe Lugach is the man you sent, or maybe you just think he is. I don't know that, either. All I know is you've got no right to steal him, or abuse him. And if you were telling the truth, seems like you wouldn't do those things. You'd identify the man, return him to his family, be honest about it."

"And let everybody know the story? Let every greedy fool in the galaxy go hunting for the Heartworld and perhaps even find it, before I know myself where it is? Oh no. No. You haven't any idea what's involved, Chattan. It isn't merely the tracking down of a legend. Think what scientific knowledge our forefathers must have had, to tame a galaxy! Think what we could learn…"

"For the benefit of Interstellar Research?" asked Chattan, and Harvey laughed.

"Naturally. Inevitably. Suppose *you* found the Heartworld, Chattan, with all that treasure of knowledge. What could you do with it?"

"Give it to the galaxy."

"Yes," said Harvey patiently, "but how? Through whom, through what agency? How would you study it, how would you safeguard it, how would you keep out the dishonest and the ignorant?"

"I don't know," said Chattan stubbornly, "but I am not going to help you steal Lugach away from the carnival."

HARVEY'S MOUTH tightened into a thin straight line. Chattan was beginning to know that look too.

"The man belongs to me," said Harvey quietly. "That which is written on his body belongs to me, and only I can read it. Listen to me carefully, Chattan, once more. I will dismiss the charge against you. I will pay you any sum you may ask, within reason, and I will see to it that you have a life-long job in my organization. And all you have to do in return is to get the man you call Lugach away from the carnival and bring him to me. He trusts you. It shouldn't be hard."

"No," said Chattan, "just impossible. Like you said, he trusts me. So do the others. So go to hell."

"The man needs medical attention," said Harvey, his voice now almost inaudible. "Do you want him to remain an idiot, a hapless freak for fools to gawk at? I can give him the best doctors, the best psychiatrists. I can cure him."

"The kind of treatment you were giving him in the alley he can do without," said Chattan. "And anyway, I don't believe a word of this stuff. You're the one needs the psychiatrists, Harvey."

Harvey reached out and struck Chattan with his open hand, back and forth.

"You're not very bright," he said. "You haven't grasped the situation at all. You talk as though you had a choice."

He turned away, and Barbour and VanFleet stepped in. It was their turn again.

Play it rough. Barbour with the swollen nose, VanFleet with the sore gut. Play it rough, and love it.

"We can boost the charge against you. It's felonious assault now, but we can swear to anything. We can make it attempted murder. We can put you where you'll never see sunlight again as long as you live."

Punctuation marks, shaped with fists. Walls, floor, ceiling, bare and whirling with unsteady pace. Blood, salt-sweet in his mouth, hot and wet running down his chin, out of his nose, from around his eyes.

"What do you care about that idiot? What does he mean to you, why are you so hot to protect him? Do you know something about him, Chattan? Something you're not telling? A clue to the Heartworld? Has he talked? What's behind you, Chattan? Who's behind you?"

"Didn't you hear? He can't be bought. He's noble, that's all. He's not dirty, like us."

One of them, somebody, hit him in the side. Chattan screamed and darkness flowed over him, wrapping him, hiding him. He wanted it to stay dark, but then a light came, a pitiless light to strip him naked and show everybody where he was. He opened his eyes again. A battery lamp glared from the floor, throwing humped black shadows high against the walls, up onto the ceiling, across the high window. Looking up, Chattan thought he saw a face peering through the window, but he knew it was only his imagination because it vanished when he looked straight at it.

Harvey's turn again.

"Why not be sensible, Chattan? If you're telling the truth, if you really have no interest in this man, except for his welfare, why stand in his way and in your own? Prison for you, a life of mental darkness for him…"

Chattan tried to speak, and couldn't, and shook his head.

Barbour lifted his head up almost affectionately, and smiled, and said, "And it's all for nothing, anyway, because we'll get him. With you or without you, we'll get him."

"I wouldn't help you bastards get hold of a yellow cur pup," Chattan mumbled, and tried to bite the wrist of the hand that was holding him.

The single flimsy door into the room exploded inward without warning. A very tall, broad man rushed through it and caught Barbour up like a small boy in his enormous hands and flung him bodily into VanFleet. At almost the same instant a small and agile form covered with bright fur sprang down from the high window and settled on Harvey's shoulders and rode him shrieking to the floor. Chattan stared at them. Shemsi and Lute, he thought, from the *Merry Andrew,* but of course that isn't possible and I'm dreaming…

Shemsi's great white arms, columns of steel and marble, crashed down upon the heads of Barbour and VanFleet, crash, crash, and their faces went slack and their bodies limp. Lute, clinging to the writhing, wild-eyed Harvey, cried out something about a gun, and Shemsi went over and hit Harvey on the head, and it was suddenly very quiet and peaceful in the room. Preek came in and began to cut Chattan loose from the chair.

Chattan stared at them, still not believing. How beautifully it all fits, he thought. Preek the sensitive, he found out where I was through ESP, and brought the others to help. How clever you can be in dreams. The black shadows danced on the walls and the ceiling, and he felt cold and tired. Someone was shaking him. "Please," he said. "Please let me sleep a while."

Somebody jammed a flask into his mouth and poured drops of liquid fire down his throat. He came to again in a hurry. Preek said. "Take a little more; that's it. Now we've got to go. Stand up."

Chattan stood. Shemsi and Lute came from where they had been tying up Harvey and the others. Shemsi put his arm around Chattan. "They'll keep for a little while," he said, "with any luck. But they're going to be awfully mad when they do wake up."

They started out of the room, with Chattan wobbling in the grip of Shemsi's arm.

"They're cops," he said. "Real cops. They're bought, but nobody knows that but the three of them. They can make trouble for you."

"We know it," Preek said.

"That was Laurence Harvey," Chattan said, staggering down a long dusty hall. "Interstellar Research. Rich. Crazy. He'll…"

"Make trouble," Preek said. "We know. I'm a sensitive, remember? Save your breath, and hurry."

"Ought to let me go," Chattan said. "If I'm not with the carnival, they…"

Shemsi shook him gently. "Didn't you hear? Preek said shut up."

Lute peered out the front door and nodded. They went out into the night.

THE HOUSE TO WHICH Harvey had brought Chattan stood in an isolated and untenanted little clump of structures due, according to signs, to be razed for the construction of a new warehouse…a chemical warehouse, belonging significantly to Interstellar Research. They went away from there as fast as they could, through a tangle of dark alleyways between warehouses already built.

34

"Betta's waiting," Preek said, as they ran. "She hired a ground car, and we got as close as we dared... There it is."

A battered rental-agency vehicle, without lights, showed dimly under the shadow of a wall. Betta got out of it. She was wearing some kind of a wrap, and, underneath it there was a glint of bangles and bare flesh. She must have left the pitch without changing her costume. "Did you get him?" she said. "Good. Good. All right, let's go."

They fairly flung themselves into the car, and Preek took the controls. "I can go faster," he said. "I can see what's around the corners."

He drove, making the streets spin behind them, a broken pattern of dark and light, empty and crowded, noisy and still. Scraps of music and laughter clung to them briefly, then dropped away, Chattan looked at the back of Betta's head.

"Thanks," he said. "But I don't see why..."

"Preek couldn't stand it any longer," she said. "He could feel them beating you, and you were holding out in spite of it, and it seemed like the only thing to do."

Preek giggled suddenly. "That's only part of the truth. Why don't you tell the rest of it?"

"Just tend to your driving," Betta said.

Chattan's head had cleared enough that he could think a little. And he did not like the shape of his first thought, at all.

"You're in trouble," he told Betta. "Shemsi... Lute...the whole carnival. You took a prisoner away from authorized police, and tied them up. Harvey will crucify you for this."

Betta nodded, without turning. "I expect he'll try."

"Oh, damn it, Betta, you didn't have to all go out on a limb for me," said Chattan. "Harvey's crazy, but he's powerful, and..."

She turned around, at that. "Listen, Joe. You were the one who went out on that limb...for Lugach. What were we supposed to do... leave you out there?"

Preek went around another corner fast, and Chattan reminded himself never to ride with an esper driver again. They went past the soaring starport lights and towers, and then the small, tinselly, gaudy patch of lights that was the carnival came into view.

Business appeared to be good. Doc Brewer had a happy look about him as he came to meet them, but it was a slightly irritated look too.

"Listen," he started in, "don't you know better than to run out between shows and..." Then he stared. "Why Joe Chattan. What the hell happened to your face?"

Chattan brushed that aside. "I'll explain that later. I don't think we've got too much time."

"Come in the office-wagon," Betta said. "I've got a first-aid kit there. Might as well fix your face while we talk."

In the crowded little wagon, they talked, and as they talked Doc Brewer's happy look left him.

"Harvey, of Interstellar Research? And he saw Shemsi and Lute and Preek? Then we're sunk," he said dismally.

"Would you rather I'd left Joe there?" Betta asked.

Brewer exploded. "Hell, no! If I'd known what was up I'd have gone with you for him. But what are we going to do now? Those three won't stay tied up forever."

"By morning, they'll be yelling for the Port Police," Chattan said. "As for what you're going to do, there're two things you can do. You can give Lugach to Harvey. I'm pretty sure that'd smooth over everything."

He thought for a moment that Doc Brewer was going to hit him. "Give poor witless Lugach to that bastard? Why..." Then he stopped, and said, "What's the other thing we can do?"

Chattan had been thinking. His mind was not too clear yet but he had at least got hold of one idea, and it came from the words that had passed between him and Harvey in that room.

He said, "You can load up the show and pull out of here right now, tonight."

"Pull out for where? A man with Harvey's influence can run us down and have us arrested anywhere we go!"

Chattan said, "You told me that the captain who sold you Lugach found him on Algol One. Do you know just where he got him there?"

"Sure," said Doc Brewer, "he bought him from one of those plunder-merchants there, a man named Farah..." He stopped suddenly, and looked shocked. "You don't mean, go *there?*"

"Their warrants wouldn't run at Thieves' Star," Chattan reminded. "It'd give us time. The way I see it, Lugach is the key. Find out who Lugach really is, why Harvey really wants him, and I'm betting we'll uncover enough to tear Harvey wide open and clear ourselves. He sure isn't after Lugach because he believes in the Old Heartworld myth!"

Brewer looked thoughtful.

"Thieves' Star is a tough place to tackle, especially with our money running out. But you're right, they couldn't arrest us there." A speculative gleam came into his eye. "And if Lugach is that valuable to Harvey, it ought to be valuable to *us* to go there and find out why."

Preek spoke up unexpectedly. "You are wrong about one thing, Joe."

"I am? What?"

"Harvey *does* believe that Lugach is the key to the Heartworld. He believes in the Heartworld, utterly. In his mind, I read it."

Chattan was astounded. "Oh, no, you must have been wrong, Preek. He's too clever to chase myths."

"He believes," said Preek.

They stared at each other. Doc Brewer mopped his suddenly damp brow, and said, "What the devil have I got into, anyway? The Heartworld, is it? We'd better get out of here, and we'd better get damned fast!"

CHAPTER FIVE

THE *MERRY ANDREW* raced clumsy and creaking, toward Algol. Its clearance papers, hastily made out with the Port Authority on Sirius Five, gave Canopus as its destination, but then nobody who was headed for the Thieves' Star ever admitted it.

Algol was a curiously anomaly in those days of Galactic Federation, and a thorn in the side of galactic law…a rogue star whose worlds had chosen to remain independent, outside the Federation and free of any of its codes and contracts. They did not recognize any law but their own, and they laughed at extradition. The result was that the worlds of Algol were probably the richest in the galaxy, for the least amount of exertion. The loot and plunder of a galaxy came here to be sold in the biggest thieves' market in history. Countless men, their pockets heavy with ill-gotten fortunes, came for a healthful change of climate. The Algolians smiled, and raked in the profits.

"A devil of a place," complained Doc Brewer, "for practically honest people to be going. It's as good as admitting we're guilty of something."

"Well," said Betta crossly, "what else could we have done? We'd be behind bars now, and we could rot there for all Harvey cares. At least this way we'll have time to try and find out what's behind all this."

"If Harvey doesn't catch up with us first," said Brewer.

"We'll be on even terms with him if he does," said Chattan. "He doesn't have the law at Algol, nor his corporation, to back him up."

"He's still got money," said Brewer, "and that's good anywhere."

Over in the corner Preek swore irritably. "How do you expect me to do anything with all this babble going on? This is work for a Class One esper in the first place, and I'm only a Class Three. Give me a break, please."

They fell silent watching Preek. Shemsi and Lute were there too, and Gurtharn the animal man, holding one of his smaller charges like an ailing baby in his arms. Preek sat in front of Lugach, who was in his usual place, in his usual attitude of silent brooding.

"I can't deep-probe him," Preek said." A Class Three is frankly just not good enough. But I might be able to get something that would help us, if I could slip down through the top layer of his mind. You've no idea what a mess it is... cloudy gray, with slashes of color, mostly red, and full of outlines you can't quite see, like houses in a fog."

He shook his head. "It feels different, though, somehow, from the first time."

"What first time?" asked Chattan.

"Well, when Doc brought him aboard I took a sort of a fast survey of him. I didn't see anything then but fog, and I'm not sure I do now, but it seems thinner."

Preek settled his shoulders. His eyes got vague and unfocused. At first he was quiet, and the room was quiet, so that even the sounds of breathing seemed loud. Chattan glanced at Betta and she smiled nervously and dropped her gaze. Lute fidgeted, his small restless body shifting audibly. Gurtharn stroked the bug-eyed ball of fur in his arms.

Then Preek began to talk.

"Gray. Clouds running, coiling. Hiding. Warm, full belly, no physical pain, but the red color is fear. Behind the cloud is fear, is danger, is pain, is dead-living flayed tortured *I…*"

Preek's face contracted in a grimace of anguish. Sweat gleamed on his skin. He sat rigid and did not speak again.

Now Betta looked at Chattan, and at Doc Brewer, with increasing uneasiness. Lute stopped fidgeting. They waited.

Preek whimpered. His eyes closed and he swayed on the chair. Chattan half started to his feet. And then as though the intrusion of Preek's mind into the clouded mists of his own had triggered some fateful reaction beyond anyone's understanding. Lugach flung up his head and looked at something that was not within the iron confines of the room. He looked at it as a sane man looks upon a recognized and dreadful shape, and then he raised his hands as though to shield himself, and cowered back, and shouted…two words, three words, then nothing, and his mouth froze in the act of screaming.

Preek fell off the chair. He rolled over feebly, shook his head, and began to crawl away from Lugach. His face was white.

Doc Brewer was on his feet. "What did he say? What did he say?"

"I don't know what he said," Preek muttered, "but I know what he was thinking." He fetched up against the opposite bulkhead and sat there, panting. "I pushed. I pushed real hard, to get down past the clouds, and I guess I don't know enough about this business, or I can't control it right, because I think I opened up a way for him, too."

"Well, what was it?" demanded Doc Brewer. "What did you see?"

"A star," said Preek. "Green. Evil. Deadly. Coming to kill me." He got unsteadily to his feet. "The hell with that.

I'll never go in his mind again. I'm just a poor little Class Three, and I want to live."

He went out of the room. Betta had gone over to Lugach. She was standing helplessly beside him, her hand poised in mid-air over his shoulder. Lugach himself was doubled up now, shivering, his hands covering his head.

Chattan, feeling wretched, as though he had witnessed the torturing of an animal, went over to Lugach and bent down. He put his hands on the dark shoulders with the enigmatic silver marks, and said, gently, "Lugach... It's all right, it's all gone now. You're quite safe, Lugach."

And suddenly, the black anguished eyes were looking straight into his, and the tattooed hands were making a violent gesture of negation.

"Lugach," he said, two or three times, coupled with unintelligible words. He spoke urgently, as though it was imperative that Chattan understand, saying *Lugach* and then the words in whatever language was native to him, possibly the same language in which Harvey had spoken to him in the alley. Chattan said, "I'm sorry, I don't understand. Lugach...?"

THE DARK MAN THUMPED himself on the chest and said, "Shoba Ruk! Shoba Ruk!", and for a moment Chattan felt like a small boy reprimanded for his stupidity. He said in Universal, "Your name is Shoba Ruk."

And in clear, perfectly articulated Universal, the dark man said, "Yes, that is my name. Lugach is danger great danger if I die someone should know. Someone should know. Not Laurence." He leaned toward Chattan. "Not Laurence. That would be folly as great as theirs. Help me to...to tell..."

"Oh, Lord," said Chattan, "he's slipping away again." He caught Shoba Ruk and shook him. "Tell what? What do you want? I'll help..."

But Shoba Ruk slipped, quite literally, out of his hands and fell on the deck and lay there, breathing heavily, but otherwise still.

They looked at him, and at each other.

"He's fainted," Betta said. "Too much of a shock. I hope we haven't hurt him. Preek never meant…"

"Do you suppose we better try and bring him around?" Brewer asked.

"I think," said Chattan hesitantly, "we'd better just let him alone." In spite of his concern for Lugach or Shoba Ruk, he could not help a sense of tremendous excitement. "He did speak though… really speak. That proves he wasn't always an idiot. And he said Laurence. Did you hear?"

They had.

"Say it *was* Laurence Harvey he meant," said Doc Brewer. "What did he mean? What shouldn't Laurence know? And what's all that stuff about the green star and danger, danger? It sounds crazy to me!"

Chattan didn't answer that at once. He bent over Shoba Ruk and said, "Shemsi, will you give me a hand? We ought to get him to his bunk…"

"I'll do it," Shemsi said, and picked up the unconscious man as though he had no weight at all. "We'll take turns to watch by him," he said, and went out, with Lute tagging after.

Gurtharn, holding the little animal tenderly between his great hands, looked after Shoba Ruk and said quietly, "I think he's hiding from himself, in his own mind. When Preek began to wake his memory, he was afraid and went unconscious. Like this little one, when life is too much for him, and I find him dead in his cage and must comfort him and coax him to come alive again."

The creature narrowed its big round eyes and bit him happily on the finger, and Gurtharn laughed.

Chattan came back to Doc Brewer. He said, "So it sounded crazy to you. I don't think so. I think maybe Preek just gave you the key to a pot of gold."

"How so?"

"The green star. Doesn't it all add up? Laurence Harvey, Shoba Ruk, expedition, some discovery Harvey is frantic to get his hands on, something Shoba Ruk doesn't think he ought to have, something at or near a green star. Something valuable."

Betta caught her breath and said, "Do you think it might really be the Heartworld?"

"Harvey believes it. Preek said so. That's what he sent Shoba Ruk out to find. I'm beginning to think we'd better keep at least an open mind."

Doc Brewer swore. "Well," he said, "I'm damned. No. No, it isn't possible, and I'll tell you why. I've billed that son of a gun all over the galaxy as the Man from the Heartworld, and I've never told the truth yet on a billing. It's a tradition with me."

Remembering suddenly something Harvey had said, Chattan asked. "Why *did* you bill him that way, Doc? You must have had a reason."

"Sure I did. That tattooing. Didn't you ever hear the story, about how the real men of the Heartworld took to marking their hides in a special way nobody else could duplicate, so they'd be known anywhere they went, and so nobody could pretend to be one that wasn't? I guess that would have been after there were plenty of colonists around. Anyway, when I saw the way Luga... I mean, Shoba Ruk now, was marked, that was the first thing popped into my head. I supposed actually some tribe way back on a system you never heard of had done it, but it seemed like a safe enough lie. I never figured it might be the truth."

He thought about it a minute, and then he said, "Aw, it can't be. I just can't believe it. That fairy tale?"

Betta said, frowning, "We do know Shoba Ruk himself isn't from the Heartworld. Even if he did find it, why would *he* be tattooed?"

"I don't know," Chattan admitted. "But Harvey said he could read what was written on his skin. Well, maybe we can find out more when we hit Algol, and maybe Shoba Ruk might still be able to tell us. But I know one thing."

"What's that?" asked Doc. "As if I didn't know."

"Shoba Ruk doesn't want Laurence to have something, and I don't want him to have it either. Because whatever it is Laurence is trying to steal it, and he's scared witless that some word of the find will leak out before he can do that."

CHATTAN WAS SUDDENLY beginning to see sense behind Harvey's wild behavior.

"Say it is the Heartworld that Shoba Ruk found. That would belong to the whole galaxy, wouldn't it? The Federation government would take it over, protect it, administer it, and see to it that any scientific secrets found there were properly handled. Am I right?"

"Perfectly," said Brewer.

"Well, then, Harvey's problem is simple. If he wants to take all that scientific knowledge for himself, he's got to get there before anyone else knows about it, and before the Federation can step in. To do that, he's willing to commit any crime from kidnaping to murder, and as long as we've got Shoba Ruk we're front and center in the firing line."

"So?"

"So as I see it, the only way to save our necks, and incidentally keep Harvey from the biggest steal in history, is find that green star before he does and then scream to the Federation."

"Yes," said Doc Brewer, smiling slowly, "that sounds pretty good. It would make us heroes, with knobs on. And more important, I can think of at least forty ways it could make us rich."

"I'll bet you can," said Betta, and shook her head. "I'll buy your idea, Joe, but I'll tell you... I don't think we've got a hope of finding that star unless Shoba Ruk himself comes to and tells us."

He did not. And two days later by the ship's chronometer, they raised the white blaze of Algol and edged their way into that triple system, leaving the more distant sun to starboard and passing well above the other half of the eclipsing binary, Algol's "dark" companion that was itself almost as bright as their own remembered Sol. Presently in that overwhelming sea of radiance they picked up a planet glittering like a diamond, and settled in for a landing on Algol One.

It was a hot heavy planet, and a stormy one. It was pouring a mighty rain when the *Merry Andrew* landed, and the roar of the run-off into the underground drains was deafening when the motors stopped.

"I'll leave it to you," Doc Brewer said to Betta, "to see that the show is set up, ready for tonight. We're about broke from running out on our last pitch, and besides, it'll look better if we act normal." He stopped and looked into the cabin where Shoba Ruk lay in his bunk. His eyes were open, but he seemed if anything more distant and beyond human communication than ever. Shemsi and Lute were there.

"You watch him," Doc Brewer said. "Don't let him go out, and don't show him."

Shemsi nodded. Brewer and Chattan and Preek went on to the lock. Chattan, feeling that they might need all the help they could get, had suggested taking, the sensitive along.

45

They climbed down the ladder and stood in the roaring, pouring rain. "It'll let up soon," said Brewer. "Come on, let's get on to Farah's."

Doc led the way off the starport and into the city. The rain stopped as suddenly as though someone had turned off the tap. The double sun came out and Chattan gasped with the light and heat. Instantly a million signs, banners, flags, and pennants hung over a million doorways took fire in an explosion of color. They were in the bazaar quarter...or perhaps more correctly they were in the bazaar that was itself a giant city.

Thieves' bazaar, heaped with the loot of a galaxy, and not one item there honestly come by. Chattan had heard all about it from spacemen, but now that he saw it he didn't believe it. The vast rambling honeycomb of buildings, in every conceivable material from native stone to gaudy plastic, held such hoards of rare and wonderful things that the eye was dazzled by the ever-shifting pattern of shape and color, the glitter of gems in a dark barred window, the richness of furs and fabrics from distant worlds, objects of art beautiful, grotesque, reflecting a million different tastes. Curios, drugs, human merchandise...everything brought a price on Algol One. Chattan knew, and was not surprised, that many a respectable firm had dealings with this thieves' market.

Doc Brewer stopped at a meeting of four main ways, looking up and down. "That's the street of the drug-sellers," he said, muttering to himself, "and what's down that way I don't know, but...yes, the place we want must be up ahead."

He started on again, and Chattan said, "For somebody that hasn't been here before, you seem to know your way pretty well."

Doc Brewer said uncomfortably, "To tell you the truth, I was here once, an awful long time ago. I wasn't much more than a kid. For Pete's sake, don't tell Betta. She knows too much about my shortcomings as it is."

They went a little further, panting and steaming in the heat. Two or three times now Brewer stopped to ask directions, and presently they came into a square roofed over against the sun with crimson silk. On one side was a broad doorway with a sign that said simply, FARAH'S. Inside it was dark and cool and quiet. There were a few things around on stands and in niches, which even to Chattan's uneducated eye were obviously treasures. There was nobody in sight when they came in, and they hesitated, looking around. And suddenly Preek said in a whisper, shivering.

"There is someone watching us, with the eye of a hunting leopard."

Hangings parted at the back of the room, and a man from Fomalhaut, as white and slender and graceful as a fine blade, and with exactly the eye Preek had mentioned, nodded to them, and said, "I am Farah."

Doc Brewer began to talk, and Farah listened. Chattan tried to watch Farah's face, but the light was too dim to show any shades of expression, so he couldn't judge whether or not Farah was lying when he said, "Offhand I do not remember such a man. You're sure your friend bought him from me."

"He was definite. Yes."

"Hm. Well, it's possible. So many things pass through my hands. A tattooed man, you say? An idiot? How long ago? Let me get my records. They will show exactly, all the details."

FARAH TURNED and went out again, swiftly. Once more they stood in the quiet room, uneasy, waiting. And once more Preek spoke, in a hurried undertone.

"That man is a thief and a liar. His mind is a maze... I get lost in it. Blood... he kills easily, for profit, not for pleasure. And now..."

"Isn't he getting the records?" asked Brewer.

"Yes, but there are others with him. Damn! If I could only see more clearly... He's sending them away, they're going away, and Farah's mind is busy reckoning..."

"Reckoning what?" asked Chattan.

"Money," said Preek. "And bodies. Ours."

Farah came back with a microbook spool and clipped it into a viewer.

"Now let's see," he said. "It would have been about this time... yes, here it is. Adult male, origin unknown, distinguishing marks... yes, yes, I remember now." Farah smiled. "He had the word Lugach tattooed on his hands, and he was a complete idiot. I bought him as a favor from a friend of mine who was hard up, and resold him at a fair profit to your friend."

Very carefully Doc Brewer said, "Do you happen to remember where your friend got him?"

Farah seemed honestly to be thinking. "Somewhere in space, I think. I seem to remember something about a lifeboat..."

"Would you," asked Brewer, trying to keep his voice steady, "remember about where in space?"

Farah shook his head. "I'm afraid not," he said, and laughed. "It hardly seemed important. But, if it's important to you, I can try to find out. Of course, my time is valuable to me..."

"We'll be very happy to pay you," Brewer said. "It is important to us...sort of a, uh, personal matter."

"Give me a day or two," Farah said, "Where can I reach you?"

Doc Brewer told him, and they went out again, into the heat that did not seem to be diminishing in spite of the lowering sun.

"What did you think?" asked Brewer, and Chattan grunted.

"That's a man I wouldn't turn my back on. Still, he's probably telling the truth. How about that, Preek?"

"Truth," said Preek absently. "Yes. But let's go that way, around the corner."

Brewer protested, but turned, and then at Preek's urging they doubled twice more in the maze of winding streets.

"Those men he sent out of his place," said Preek finally. "They're following us."

The shadows were long in the streets of the thieves' bazaar. Overhead the signs and the banners blazed in the slanting light. Men went by, soft-footed, sharp-eyed, and every one of them was potentially an enemy.

Chattan said, "Where?"

"Just around that last corner."

"Okay," said Chattan. "Doc, you walk on, like you're walking now, straight ahead. Preek, you see that opening there between those shops? Right under green banner with the sunburst on it. When we get there, you and I will turn in."

"I don't like to separate," Doc protested.

"You won't have to go far. Down to the next square, and wait." The alley mouth was beside them now, narrow and dark between the building walls. The huge banner rustled overhead. Chattan and Preek turned into it. When they were out of sight of the street they ran, over the crooked stones, until the uneven line of the wall gave them a niche to hide in. There were doors and windows unevenly spaced. Lights showed in some of them, and somewhere, languidly, a woman was singing.

"Quiet," murmured Preek, pressing nervously against the wall. "One is going on with Doc. The other's turning in."

The shadows grew thicker in the crooked lane, Chattan stood still, waiting, his head turned so that his cheek touched the warm, crumbling plaster.

Footsteps came, light and wary, across the stones.

Chattan shifted his weight, drawing a slow breath.

A man came into sight, moving very cautiously, looking from side to side. He saw Chattan at the same instant Chattan saw him. He stopped short and his hand flew to his belt, but Chattan was on him before he had time either to draw or run.

CHAPTER SIX

THE MAN WAS LEAN and wiry and vicious. He did not want to be held. He gave Chattan the knuckles of his two fists in a double uppercut, and the point of one bony knee in the belly. Chattan pulled his head back so the doubled fists just grazed his forehead, and the knee he managed to slide off onto one hip. He was angry, angry at being followed, at being pushed around, at being made the goat for other people's plans, at the whole mess he had got into through one simple act of mercy. He hit the wiry man. He hit him hard.

"Now, then," he said, "Why are you following us?"

Black eyes glared, dazed and furious, out of a brown face, Chattan shook him.

"Farah sent you. Why?"

"You ask him. I'm only a hired boy," gasped the wiry man. "He doesn't tell me why. Let me go."

"Not until I find out…"

"*Watch* it!" said Preek suddenly, but it was too late. The wiry man had got his breath back and begun to yell.

"Thieves!" he yelled. "Murder! Help!" His voice shrilled and echoed from the crowding walls. "Shut up," said Chattan fiercely. "Shut up!" But the damage was already done. Heads appeared in windows and doors opened.

"Let him go," Preek said. "He doesn't know, anyway. For godsake, let's get out of here."

Chattan gave the man a final blow to shut his mouth, and then he and Preek ran back along the alley and into the street again. They slowed to a fast walk and caught up finally with Doc, who was waiting anxiously at the next square. Pursuit, if any, was left behind.

"As near as I could get from his mind," Preek said, "he thought we were queer people to be dealing with Farah, and he figured Farah thought so, too. Maybe that's true. I suppose we did look a little funny coming in there asking questions about a tattooed idiot."

"Is the other one still with us?" asked Chattan.

"Like a mother."

Chattan contemplated further action, but gave it up. "We wouldn't get any more from him than we did from the first one. And I suppose in Farah's line of work it's automatic to be suspicious of people you don't know. Just the same, damn it. I don't like to be spied on."

"Well," said Doc Brewer uneasily. "I don't either, but I reckon we'll have to put up with it until tomorrow, anyway. Farah might know something by then, and anyway, we won't have money enough to buy fuel to get the *Merry Andrew* off until after the show. Maybe not then, if business isn't good. But I guess it might be a wise idea to keep guard on Lugach every minute."

They went on back to the ship. And night came on slowly, with hot winds and a burning radiance of stars,

Betta had done a good job setting up the show. Many-colored lights danced in the wind, splashing the plastic tents with glimmers of green and gold and red. Betta, in silver spangles, was doing her come-on...an acrobatic sort of dance involving rings, bars, and a padded platform. She was only moderately good at it, but her lithe little figure and bright personality brought the customers' in. After a while, when she had them softened up a bit, Shemsi came out and tossed her around, gently and with splendid ease, so that she looked like a silver leaf whirling high among the lights. The crowd, half tolerant, half openly scornful but with a what-the-hell-it's-something-to-do expression; began to buy tickets and pass in. Doc Brewer held up crossed fingers.

"It looks like a good night," he said in the tone of one too often betrayed

Chattan agreed that it did. But the hot wind ruffled his hair the wrong way and the ground felt wrong when he walked on it, and all the familiar shapes of ship and carnival grounds were somehow changed and threatening. Nerves, he thought, and strolled back and forth, but the feeling didn't leave him. He went inside the *Merry Andrew* and checked on Lugach, or Shoba Ruk...having got used to one name, it was hard to change. He remembered Laurence Harvey's voice saying, the oldest names for the Heartsworld are *Lludoc, Lukah, Hludag. Lugach. W*as it possible, really, that the name tattooed on the hands of Shoba Ruk was the true name of the lost cradle of humankind?

Shoba Ruk still lay in his bunk. Shemsi and Lute were busy with their performances, and the cook and his helper were standing guard.

"He's quiet enough," said the cook, "but he's been talking. To himself. I couldn't make any sense of it. Nekru here thought he recognized the language, but he wasn't sure, and..."

CHATTAN SWUNG on the helper so intently that the man was startled. He was a long gray lazy man, from one of the nameless star systems that dot the hinterlands of the galaxy much as the nameless villages filled the hills and the wide plains of Earth in the old days. The natives had names for them, but outside them nobody cared.

"Did you understand it?" Chattan demanded.

"No, sir," said Nekru. "I only said I thought it sounded like the way a man I worked with once used to talk, and he looked like this fellow, too. Only had his wits, of course, and he wasn't tattooed. But otherwise he looked like him. Same color. Not that that means anything by itself."

"No," said Chattan, digging his nails into the palms of his hands, "but if they looked alike and spoke alike it might mean something. Where did this other man come from?"

"Some little star system way over beyond Eridanus. I can't remember the name…"

"Please?" said Chattan. "Try."

Nekru looked at him, and then frowned in an agony of effort. "Thir. Thir-something. I think. It was a long time ago. Thirban? Thirbar? Something like that."

And that was the best he could do, Chattan went and leaned over the bunk. "Shoba Ruk," he said. "Shoba Ruk."

The eyes of the dark man flickered. He muttered something in his own language.

"I can't understand you, Shoba Ruk," said Chattan. "Is your home at Thirban?"

Again the dark man muttered. Then he moved his head impatiently and spoke in Universal. "Thirbar, Thirbar. Yes. Now leave me. I am very busy."

Chattan leaned closer. "Shoba Ruk…where is Lugach?"

Instantly he was sorry. The long gaunt body in the bunk became agitated, and the face was convulsed. "Lugach," whispered Shoba Ruk, and lifted his hands. "If I write it there I will remember someday if I live, the sight in my eyes, the sound in my ears repeated. Must remember! Danger if…"

He reached up and caught Chattan by the front of his jacket. His eyes blazed.

"Laurence, this power is not for one man. I forbid you. You are like them, greedy, proud, and stupid. Old stubborn parents who would not let go the swaddling bands. Stupid, stupid, pitiful, and you're like them. You must not."

He let go and sank back, smiling. "Anyway, you can't. You have not the key of entrance to the vault. And the green star kills. I only am left alive."

His eyes closed, and then a minute later he opened them again and said testily, "I am busy. These things must come in order, don't you understand that? Get out. Get out."

Chattan stepped back from the bunk. The cook and Nekru were staring, scared but fascinated. Chattan's heart was pounding.

"Watch him," he said. "Every minute. And if he says anything you can understand, for God's sake remember it."

He ran out of the cabin, out of the ship, back to the carnival pitch where the red and green and yellow lights danced in the hot wind, and the good-paying crowd pushed among the bright-colored booths, and the recorded music gave out sounds of brassy cheerfulness. He looked for Doc Brewer, and found him in the office wagon, counting the take.

"Pretty good," said Doc. "We can buy fuel…"

"I've got something better," Chattan said. He told him briefly what Shoba Ruk had said. "I think he's coming round, back to sanity. He's having to do it his own way, slowly, remembering things, and trying to arrange them properly.

There ought to be someone with him now all the time, with a tape recorder to take down everything he might say. I think..."

Abruptly, with the suddenness of a blow, the lights went out.

There was a second of absolute silence. Then Doc Brewer said, "The generator...", and in the same moment all over the carnival pitch voices rose, dismayed and querulous. Chattan jumped down from the wagon. The portable generator was close by, and he started toward it in the dark. To his right he could make out the curving row of booths and the massed yeasty movement of people. The music had stopped with the lights, and there was no sound but the voices and the trampling of feet.

He heard Doc Brewer come out of the wagon and go toward the booths, calling out that everything was all right, just a little generator trouble, nothing to worry about. Then a woman screamed with the sharp insistence of real fear. A man's voice took it up with a cry of, "Look out!" Then, on top of those two voices, smothering and crushing them down, an avalanche of noise descended...howls, shouts, the cries of frightened animals, the stamping of feet and the crashing of falling things, with an obligato of female screaming above it all.

Doc Brewer came back, running. He ran into Chattan, saw who it was, and pulled him on. "For God's sake get the lights back on."

"What is it, a panic?"

"It's one now, all right, but it sounds like a clem to me."

"What's that?"

"Fight. Raid. Where the natives come in and wreck you. Hear that?"

SPLINTERING CRASHES, bellows, sounds of rage and turmoil. Chattan thought he could hear Shemsi's great voice. The portable generator loomed in the night in front of him, housed in its own bright plastic hut. It was not working. Doc Brewer stumbled over something on the ground and swore. It was the end of a cable, chopped in two.

"They've all been cut," said Chattan, He straightened up in sudden alarm. "Christ," he said. "Shoba Ruk."

"Oh lord," said Brewer. "You don't think..."

They began to run again, through the wind and the hot night, toward the *Merry Andrew*. But Chattan did not go all the way. "Let him go," he said to Brewer. "The hell with him. I'm going to find Betta."

"She's all right," Brewer said. "She knows what to do. She's been through these before."

But Chattan left him and plunged into the locked, swaying, struggling mass of people among the booths. Little herds of them broke loose and ran this way and that, knocking things over, trampling each other into the dust. There were moans and curses. Chattan saw the dim outlines of people in spangled costumes trying to lead patrons off the grounds. And now he saw others, Shemsi among them distinguishable by his great height, fighting savagely with a knot of men who were armed with clubs and bars. Chattan pushed and butted and kicked his way to the central hub of conflict. It too was moving, lurching back and forth as the tide of battle and the outward pressures of the crowd moved it. Betta's ring-and-bar set-up were wrecked, but the platform still stood firm.

Chattan shouted to Shemsi, "Where's Betta? The giant's answer was swallowed up in the noise of the fight, and so was Chattan in the physical motion of it. Bodies banged against his. Hot angry men panted and cursed in his ear. He hunched his shoulders and went at it, trying not to hit anything with spangles on it. The night became an insanely whirling mess of fists, feet, faces, clubs, and dust, all floundering over pieces of wreckage and softer things that groaned and crawled away.

Then, as abruptly as it had begun, it was over.

The men with the clubs turned and ran away. The last of the patrons were gone from the pitch, except a half-dozen injured who lay on the ground and cried. A hooting of sirens arose in the distance, coming closer. Someone had called in an alarm. Chattan stood panting and looking dizzily around. He saw Shemsi and asked again, "Where's Betta?"

"I told you she was all right," said Shemsi, and moved the wreckage away from the platform. He opened one side of it and said, "Come out now."

Betta and two of the other women performers crawled out. "Dad calls that the storm cellar," Betta said, and looked around, alarmed. "Where is Dad? He didn't get hurt?"

"He went to the ship," Chattan said. "We thought they might be after Shoba Ruk..."

They all turned toward the ship. There was no sign of life around the open hatch.

"It is funny," said Shemsi, "how quick it began and ended. And this is not the kind of place where you expect a chem."

Betta made a sharp sound between her teeth and started to run. Chattan and the others went with her.

There was a queer sweetish smell in the open lock of the ship, quite faint but getting stronger as they went along the corridor. Doc Brewer lay on the deck half in and half out of Shoba Ruk's cabin. Chattan thought at first that he was dead, but he stirred when Betta flung herself, down beside him and lifted his head, and suddenly Chattan knew what had happened.

"Knock-out gas," he said. "Get him out in the air." He shoved past Betta into the cabin. The cook and Nekru were lying on the deck there. There was nobody else in the room. Shoba Ruk was gone.

Chattan's own head was beginning to reel. A couple of those gas shells could incapacitate a whole ship's company making it perfectly safe for intruders to come in no matter how many people there might be aboard. It insured quietness, too. Very neatly done, thought Chattan, and staggered off down the corridor carrying part of the cook's dead weight with Preek.

Outside there were still no lights, but a curious crowd had built up around the edges of the pitch. And now the ground cars with the sirens on them swept in.

Chattan, working over the unconscious men, looked up at Preek and said, "Farah did this. Nobody else here even knew about Shoba Ruk, so it must have been Farah."

Preek nodded. He turned apprehensively toward the ground cars and the men who were getting out of them.

"Farah is a power here at Algol, and we are strangers. I wonder now how much justice we're due to get?"

DURING THE NEXT four days, Chattan thought they didn't get a lot. It wasn't that the authorities were openly oppressive or unfair. They were methodical and thorough, polite, and utterly immovable. There was a law on Algol One. Even a thieves' world has to have some sort of a code to keep it from falling into complete chaos. They asked endless questions, listened to endless answers, and in regard to Farah they always came back to the same remark. "But you have no evidence." Which was perfectly true.

As for Farah, he was gone. His shop was locked tight. The men on either side of it said that he had left on the evening of the day the strangers had been there. They did not know where he had gone. When Chattan asked them if Farah had a place somewhere else, they didn't know that either. Nobody knew. Every face in the city was as blank as a shuttered window, when any question was asked.

"I guess," said Doc Brewer, "our trouble is we're not crooks, and so they figure we're fair game."

"They're sure covering up for Farah," said Chattan grimly. "I tried to check with the port authority to see if he'd taken off in a ship, and they practically threw me out."

Doc Brewer looked with haggard, hating eyes at the crowded buildings of the thieves' bazaar. "Looks like poor old Lugach is gone for sure. And just when it looked as though he might come round. But what I can't figure out is this. Why did Farah want him?"

Chattan shook his head. With Preek and Shemsi and Lute he prowled the twisting streets, while Doc Brewer fought it out with the law and cleaned the pitch of its bright gay wreckage, salvaging what he could. And they got nowhere. Even Preek could not pick up anything definite. "I think Farah has a place somewhere a long way from here, and I think everyone knows pretty well where it is. I can even get a picture of a big sort of a villa with white walls and some jungly gardens around it. But that's all, and it could be anywhere. It could be on another planet."

They could not find any trace of the two men Farah had sent to trail them, either, and neither they nor the police could turn up the slightest indication of who the rioters were or how the thing had been planned. Late on the fourth day an official came, placed a formal paper in Doc Brewer's hands, nodded, and went away. The paper gave them twenty-four hours to get fueled and go.

"To prevent further trouble," Doc quoted, and swore. "Well, that's the best yet…throwing us out of this thieves' den because we're undesirable!"

"What happens if we don't go?" asked Betta.

59

"They confiscate the *Merry Andrew*, and probably end up by selling us in the bazaar." Doc's shoulders sagged. "I don't know. I don't see any help for it."

Chattan said furiously, "I'm going to make one more try. Come on, Preek."

They went back into the streets, in a downpour of rain. In bitter desperation, thinking of Shoba Ruk and the dangerous secret he guarded. Whatever it might be...thinking of Laurence Harvey and the Heartworld, and the trouble that waited for the *Merry Andrew* as soon as it came again within reach of galactic law...Chattan returned to the square where Farah's shop was, not expecting anything, not hoping, just drawn to it because it was the only focal point there was.

The canopy of crimson silk was rolled up. Rain poured into the square and ran swishing and roaring into a sunken drain. The light was dim and all the colors were grayed, and there was no one in sight. Farah's place was still shuttered, still dark.

"We might as well go," said Chattan. "There's nothing for us here."

He turned away. Preek touched his arm and said, "Wait."

A man stepped out of a doorway and joined them. He was a little man with a face like a bird, very sharp and predatory, with bright shallow eyes.

"I understand you're looking for a piece of information," he said. "I can sell it to you, if you want to buy."

Chattan reached out and caught him so he could not run away. "I'll buy," he said. "I'll buy!"

Hours later, delayed by refueling and red tape, the *Merry Andrew* took off. But the ship's course was an odd one. When it was well beyond the atmosphere it shot suddenly off on a tangent and swooped back down for a landing on the other side of the planet. There was no city here, no jumble of buildings and unseemly marts of trade. There were vast estates and garden villas, resorts set miles apart in lush jungle and lake and river, every appurtenance of the spacious and serene life. There was one particular villa with white walls, even more isolated than most. And here the *Merry Andrew* came roaring and clattering down in the private dock, its loutish and rusty bulk looking painfully out of place beside the sleek space-yacht that was already there.

Chattan and Doc Brewer left the ship, with Preek and Shemsi. Everyone else had strict orders to remain inside. They walked toward the villa.

Farah and his men met them halfway.

It was daytime here, high noon. Algol blazed in the sky. The jungle smelled moist and green and there were flowers in it, and flowers on the white walls of the house, crimson and orange. Doc Brewer looked at Farah and said, "Where's Lugach?"

Farah smiled. "Well," he said, "I'll tell you. You're a little late. Laurence Harvey's yacht took off from here this morning, with Lugach safely under hatches." He smiled broadly still, and nodded. "I'm indebted to you, really. I turned a nice, a very nice profit."

"Did you?" said Chattan, and laughed, a loud harsh sound in the green and sunlit quiet.

CHAPTER SEVEN

FARAH LOOKED at Chattan, and something flickered in his eyes. "I suppose you're angry," he said. "And I guess you have a right to be, but all's fair on Algol One. If you can't protect your property, you lose it. It's a kind of game with us, though we play it mostly with outsiders."

"It's a kind of a stupid game," said Chattan. "Don't you think?"

"We rather pride ourselves on not being stupid," Farah said, "but I'll admit I was where the idiot was concerned. That's why I was determined to make up for it. I bought him, as I told you, for very little, and sold him to your tramp skipper for what I thought then was a good price. But then later an agent of Laurence Harvey's came round and offered a fabulous sum for the creature…and you can imagine my rage. So naturally, when you came to me the other day, and I was sure you had him…"

He shrugged eloquently. "One doesn't like to be haunted by past mistakes, especially where there's money involved. I notified Harvey's agent, Harvey himself got here fast, and I held him up for even more than he had offered before. Now we are both satisfied."

Chattan said, "You poor fool. Do you know what you've done? You've given away the key to the greatest secret in the galaxy. You've handed it to Harvey on a silver platter, for buttons, for nothing. You've given him the Heartworld."

That name rang like a great bell on the silence that followed its speaking. Farah stared at Chattan, and then at Doc Brewer and Preek and Shemsi. He drew a deep breath and his mouth tightened.

"I don't think I quite understood you," he said. "Would you repeat that?"

"The Heartworld," said Chattan. "The little idiot has been there. He knows where it is."

Now it was Farah's turn to laugh. "The Heartworld? Aren't we a trifle old for fairy tales?"

"Laugh," said Chattan. "Go on, choke on it. Why do you suppose Harvey was so frantic to get hold of a tattooed idiot…for a mantel ornament?"

"He told me," Farah said slowly, "that the man was a victim of one of his Company's chemical experiments that went wrong, and he wanted to do something for him. I thought what he really meant was to put him quietly out of the way, so he wouldn't make Interstellar Research look bad…"

"And you believed that?" said Chattan. "You were easy, Farah. You were easy for Harvey."

Chattan had purpose in his taunt. He had been thinking very fast since they had found Shoba Ruk gone. He had been thinking that they had only one chance left now, and that it was in the ruthless thief before them.

They…he and Doc and the *Merry Andrew*…could not follow Harvey, for they did not know where to follow. The only lead left was in what Farah knew, or could find out. If he could play on Farah's greed and rage, the game might not be lost yet…

A very hard, cruel light had come into Farah's eyes. "I dislike to be played with, and I dislike even more to be cheated… You've aroused a doubt in my mind now. I think you'd better clear it up."

Chattan nodded toward the house. "Let's go inside. The story's too long to tell standing here."

Inside, in a long room with shaded windows and cool ceramic panels on the walls, Chattan told the story. Not all of it, but just as much as he wanted Farah to know. And Farah listened, his slim graceful body and his eyes reminding Chattan more and more of Preek's comparison to a hunting leopard.

Chattan concluded, "That's why we asked you those questions about the man. We hoped if we could find out where he was picked up, it might give us a lead to the Heartworld. We hoped we could find it first. But now…" Chattan shrugged in assumed hopelessness, "…now Harvey's got him, which means that Harvey's got the Heartworld."

Doc Brewer said, "I could kill you, Farah. Poor Lugach. I hate to think what Harvey'll do to him to make him talk."

Farah's eyes became slits of pure anger. "If you're telling me the truth," he said, "and I think you are, Harvey has robbed me of a fortune I can't even count in my mind." He made a furious gesture and sprang up. "He won't get away with it."

"It's only a sort of a game he plays," said Chattan cruelly.

Farah looked at him. "Very well. I deserve that. But the question is...what do we do now?"

"*We?*" said Chattan.

"It is in my mind," said Farah, "that we could join forces to snatch the richest prize in history out of Harvey's hands, even yet."

Chattan's heart leaped. The merchant-thief was taking the bait as he had hoped. But he made his voice dull and hopeless, as he said, "Even if we trusted you, Farah...which we don't...what could we do together? Shoba Ruk was the key to the Heartworld. And he's gone. You gave him to Harvey, remember?"

A hidden fire flashed in Farah's eyes. "Listen, Chattan. You didn't tell me everything. You got some clue from Shoba Ruk to where the Heartworld is. Didn't you?"

"We did," Chattan said bluntly, "and I didn't tell you. Anyway, it's not enough."

"But," pressed Farah, "it would be enough, if you knew also where Shoba Ruk was first picked up in space? You said that, you said that that would give you a lead to the Heartworld."

Chattan stared at him. "Now I get it. You're proposing a deal?"

"Exactly," Farah spoke with a wolf-like snap. "I can get that information, from the man who did pick up Shoba Ruk. I can also check fast with Thirbar about Shoba Ruk. If we put together what we know, we can still find the Heartworld."

CHATTAN ASSUMED a look of heavy reluctance. "I don't know. What good would it do to find it…when Harvey's ahead of us?"

"He can't be far ahead," said Farah. "And my space-yacht is even faster than his, far business reasons. We can overtake him, maybe even reach the Heartworld before him. What do you say?"

Chattan looked at Doc Brewer, who looked blankly back at him and said, "Well, I would like to get Shoba Ruk out of Harvey's hands."

Preek looked worried and unhappy, but Chattan ignored him. He had jockeyed Farah into the place where he wanted him, and now there was still a chance!

He said slowly, "All right, Farah. But two things. First, no more than two of your men go with us if we go…"

"You really *don't* trust me, do you?" said Farah, with a nasty little smile.

"That," Chattan assured him, "is an understatement. And secondly…I'll tell you what *we* know *after* we reach the region Shoba Ruk came from."

Farah thought briefly, and then nodded. "All right. I think we understand each other. I'll get busy. I don't think it'll take long…I've channels of information that even the galactic police haven't."

"We'll be in the *Merry Andrew*," said Chattan.

They went back out of the villa and into the carnival ship. And the moment they were inside, Preek burst into remonstrance. He said, "I read only one thing in Farah's mind. Treachery, treachery, treachery! *I* would not go anywhere with that man!"

Chattan nodded. "Of course. He plans to fox us if we actually find the Heartworld. We'll have to be ready and alert…first to deal with Harvey, and then with Farah."

He turned and said, "Doc, I'd rather you didn't go. Shemsi and Preek and I will be enough. You stay here with Betta."

Doc instantly told him where he could go, so angrily that Chattan said hastily, "All right, all right, come along if that's the way you feel…"

Betta turned and went out of the cabin. Chattan followed, and found her in the dingy cabin where he had first met her.

He said. "I'm sorry, Betta. But Doc will come. Don't worry, I'll look out for him the very best I can."

She turned. There were tears in her eyes. Chattan had never seen her anything but brisk and competent before and he was shocked.

She said, "That's fine. And who's going to look out for *you?* You think you're so tough, but a couple of tigers like Harvey and Farah will eat you like a lamb, and…" She turned away again. "Oh, all right, you big fool, go ahead and die or lose your wits like Lugach. Go on, all of you…"

She didn't finish, because he bent his head and kissed her and then held her so tightly that she had no more breath to talk.

"I'm crazy about you, too, Betta," he said. "But listen…we have to do this. Whatever happens about the Heartworld. We have to nail Harvey and clear ourselves or we'll be on the wrong side of the law for life."

In the next few hours it turned out that Farah did indeed have swift channels of information. Over the interstellar communication system, far faster than light or even than a ship in overdrive, came the information from Thirbar that a man named Shoba Ruk, scholar, archaeologist, and explorer, had left on an expedition to an undisclosed destination eight years before, and was missing and presumed dead. Shoba Ruk, the communique added. Was a specialist in comparative cultures and the diffusion of mythology…especially the

Heartworld myth. Thirbar was traditionally one of the first colonies, and therefore presumably fairly close to the source, Laurence Harvey, added the message, had studied under Shoba Ruk there for two years.

The other information came from closer at hand. Farah's private spy system, working through the customary channels of the thieves' world, turned-up the friend from whom Farah had bought Shoba Ruk on Algol Three.

"He remembered quite clearly," Farah said. "He found a lifeboat drifting. There were three men aboard. Two were dead. The third one was Lugach...Shoba Ruk...as near dead as you can get, partly from starvation. He took him in and fed him up, not realizing until later that the man's mind was gone. Then he sold him cheap to me, because of that tattooing."

"But where?" asked Chattan eagerly. "Where in space did he find him?"

"Beyond Eridanus. In a sector well beyond the sector of Thirbar."

Minutes later, in the chartroom of Farah's yacht, they stared with excited eyes and pounding hearts at the three-dimensional representation of that sector in the tank.

"It takes in an awful lot of space," said Doc Brewer.

But Chattan, remembering what Shoba Ruk had said, was looking for a green star. It had to be a green star.

In that sector, there were three green stars with planets. Two were well-known, prosaic systems, on the extreme edges of the sector, impossible as candidates for the lost Heartworld.

THE THIRD, ISOLATED in the deep center of the sector, was a poison star. *Lethal radiation,* said the chart. *Planetary system unexplored. At least four ships known to have perished in approach. All shipping warned to stay clear of radiation zone.*

Chattan's heart sank. How could the Heartworld be there? How could life begin on the planet of a star that was lethal to life? And yet...Shoba Ruk himself had said, "The star kills."

Farah said, "I've filled my part of the bargain. Now...where in that sector?"

Chattan knew that, even if he dared trust Farah enough to tell him, to tell him now would end it. Farah would never believe in the last possibility now left.

He said, "Oh no, not yet, Farah. Not till we reach that sector. I'll set the course."

Farah said, "So you're afraid I'll leave you behind if you tell? All right. We'll start."

While Doc went hastily to get Shemsi, Chattan went to the bridge of Farah's yacht. It was good to be on a bridge again. He had been like a fish out of water ever since that night on Rigel Two. He began the regular pre-flight check, admiring the beautiful modernity of the Control system, and trying not to think about Betta, trying to think of anything else, of Harvey and how they would get him, of Shoba Ruk and a poison star.

Farah came in, dressed in a spaceman's coverall. He said suspiciously, "I only brought two men, as you stipulated. But I've got four of you aboard. That little furry chap wouldn't let the big one go without him."

"Lute and Shemsi are great friends," Chattan said. "But if you're worried. We can still call it off."

Farah gave him a piercing look. "I wonder," he said softly, "if you're as clever as you think you are." He strapped himself into the pilot's seat. "I'll take her off. I'm used to her and she's a lot crankier than any freighter."

Warning bells rang, and Farah's hand pressed down on the control board, and the yacht screamed skyward on a trail of flame, up into the blaze of Algol and then, turning away from the triple suns, it plunged toward the starry firmament.

Unnumbered stars were a great blaze before them, the sprawling magnificence of the galactic spaces, the shining cataracts of the vast star-streams, the pulsing glow of nebulae and brooding blackness of dark clouds and lonely lighthouse sparks of far-drifted stars, all hitting the vision like a blow, Chattan thought that long and long ago the ships of the Heartworld might have sped through these same spaces, and where now were those galactic mariners of old? Lost in myth and fable, lost in shadow... and where would they be when their own voyage ended?

The warning siren for overdrive screeched, after Chattan had set a course on the computer banks for the sector that was their destination. They made the shift, and then, for a while, there was nothing to do but wait.

And talk. Chattan talked, to Doc Brewer and Shemsi and Lute, out of hearing of Farah and his two Silent, watching men. He felt a great and growing doubt, and it made him seek reassurance from them, a reassurance they could not give.

"I'm getting old, Joe," said Doc Brewer. "And I'm afraid. I'm afraid we'll never find Harvey or Shoba Ruk, that they're dead like others that tried to find the Heartworld."

"But Shoba Ruk was there," Chattan insisted. "He was there once, and came away...we know that from the name "Lugach" that was tattooed on his hands."

He had thought about that, going over it again and again, trying to understand. And he thought he understood now.

"Don't you see, Shoba Ruk must have tattooed that name on his own hands, so that if he lived to get away, the name would make him remember. Which means his memory, his mind, was beginning to go when he did it."

"But what about the other tattooing on him, the silver lines all over him?" said Doc. "He didn't do that to himself. And...if he felt his mind going, what hellish kind of place was it that he was getting away from?"

That was the thought that haunted Chattan's mind. He thought he guessed the answer to it, but he didn't want to tell that shattering answer until he had to.

Time crawled endlessly on the indicators. Chattan waited, and ate, and slept, and waited, with the bitter taste of defeat already on his tongue. It seemed to him that if Harvey had taken Shoba Ruk to the place that he thought, they must indeed already both be dead, and if that were so, the whole mad venture was useless.

The countless hours became like a strange dream. It was always like that, in overdrive, but this time more than ever before. And he almost dreaded the awakening from that dream, when it finally came.

He had made his calculations with minute care. When they did, finally, go through the cosmic turbulence of translation and ride once more in normal space, the yacht was in space not far from the baleful glare of a great green star.

Farah said, "Now where?"

Chattan nodded to the green star. "There."

Farah looked at the star, and then went and looked at the chart. His face got tight and dangerous. "That's a lethal star. Nobody can go near that. What kind of game are you playing, Chattan?"

The others had crowded into the bridge to see, and they too looked at Chattan uneasily.

Chattan said, " *You have not the key of entrance to the vault. And the green star kills. I only am left alive.*' "He added. "That's what Shoba Ruk said."

70

"But it's not possible!" cried Farah. "The radiation of that star kills, at more than planetary distances. How could anyone land on its world? How could a world of that star be the Heartworld?"

"The star," Chattan said, "may not always have been dead. They do change sometimes, you know. It may have changed, in the ages since the Heartworld."

Farah made a violent gesture. "That makes no difference to us. How can a man land there? How could Shoba Ruk have landed there?"

Chattan shook his head. "I don't know. But he said he had. He was very upset about what he found there, afraid Laurence Harvey Would find it. He mentioned a vault, and a key to it Harvey didn't have. That's all I know. But he must have found a way to beat the lethal radiation, on the way in, at least."

"On the way out, "said Doc Brewer grimly. "I guess he didn't. And that's what happened to his mind."

Farah looked long again at the distant, glaring green eye of ill omen. He said, between his teeth, "Nobody could go close to that. We've come all this way for nothing...nothing!"

RADAR AND RADIO were almost useless against the radiation that poured from the green star. They tried to locate Harvey's Yacht with them, and they could find nothing.

Farah said, "If he came here, he must have made it. Otherwise the yacht would be drifting, a derelict. *If* he came here..."

"Unless he crashed on the planet," Chattan said.

There was only one planet, as far as they could see. From where they hung in space it appeared above them, very tiny and far off, its underside flashing a cold green crescent where the light of the primary touched it. A line of shadow, pencil thin, projected outward from it, lengthening until it was lost in the surrounding dark of space.

Chattan said doggedly, "It has to be the Heartworld. And, living or dead, Harvey and Shoba Ruk are on it right now."

That thought seemed to sting Farah to fury. He cried, "But we can't land. What can we *do?*"

Chattan looked at the planet, the tiny fleck of fire trailing its shadow line. "There must be a way. Shoba Ruk made it, and he didn't have anyone to tell him how, either. Shut up and let me think."

They shut up. The yacht drifted, and Chattan watched the little far-off world move around its sun. Evil-looking child of an evil parent, he thought, and the line of the eclipse is like a black path to...

A black path.

He cried out, "The shadow! Go in along the shadow, and you have the planet itself as a shield against the radiation!"

Farah turned his head, and suddenly his eyes were hot and eager. "Of course," he said. "That must be it. It'll be tricky, running that shadow. It always is, they move so fast. But we can do it."

Chattan's belly was knotted tight inside and the palms of his hands were wet. "We'll take a vote on whether we try it."

"Vote, hell," said Farah. "We go in."

Chattan said, "You can't do it alone, Farah. And everyone here will be risking his life and sanity. I say we vote."

Farah's men, not liking it but more afraid of their boss than of the unknown menace of the star, said yes. Shemsi and Lute hung back and waited for Doc Brewer.

Brewer sweated. Greed and the nobler desire to help Shoba Ruk, and prevent Harvey from stealing God-knew-what that belonged to the people of the galaxy, told him to go ahead. Fear and common sense told him to go back.

"Do you really think it's safe?" he asked Chattan.

"Not safe. Just possible."

Brewer ran his visibly shaking hands over his face. "Oh, well," he said. "All right."

And looked as though he immediately regretted it.

Shemsi and Lute nodded, not looking very happy either. Farah said impatiently, "Satisfied?"

Chattan leaned forward. "Let's go."

The yacht swung in a wide looping curve, seeking the end of that thin shadow-line. The computers clacked, figuring the planet's orbital path and speed. Chattan fed the results to the compensator banks. He made the final check with Farah.

They shot forward, down the black path of the shadow.

And now the body of the planet was between them and the sun, a round disc of darkness quickly growing. Chattan watched it, and listened to the radiation counters, and checked the kick-blasts of the steering-jets that kept them in their narrow, ever-moving lane of safety. One moment of failure, one miscalculation, and the same thing would happen to them that must have happened to Shoba Ruk's lifeboat on its outward trip.

It occurred to him to wonder what really had happened to the original ship of that expedition, and the rest of its crew. It had seemed not improbable that it had simply crashed in landing on a wild world, but now under the circumstances Chattan was not sure. He thought that radiation might have killed them. But that did not explain how Shoba Ruk and two others had escaped.

The planetary disc grew larger, blotting out more and more of the sun. Presently it covered everything but the sullen fires of the corona, a coiling and writhing of green flames as deadly as the serpents they resembled.

And suddenly Chattan saw something, a curious ghostly gleaming that seemed to surround the planet like a phantom envelope. Before he could speak they were into it. Indicator needles jumped madly on the board, registering not radiation but energy. A brush discharge burned momentarily from every metal surface, and beyond the port a sheeting of white light flared from the hull and was gone.

"Force field!" said Chattan, and stared at Farah. "Good Lord. Do you suppose that's the answer? The whole planet shielded against the radiation?"

"It could be." The yacht plunged downward into atmosphere, into heavy air that screamed along the hull. The radiation counters remained steady. "The atmosphere hasn't been poisoned, at any rate."

"And that means, of course, that the sun wasn't always lethal, and that intelligent minds here erected a shield when it became so." Looking down at the black night side of the planet, so close now below them, Chattan shivered with a thrill of pure primitive fear.

"I wonder," he said, "if any of them are still living?"

"Who?" asked Doc Brewer.

"The First Born. If this is the Heartworld, really."

"The main thing now," said Farah, "is to find Harvey's ship. We're close enough now. Level off on standard survey pattern."

THE YACHT WENT INTO an orbital path of its own, high enough to avoid the highest possible mountain, low enough to use Scanners and detector devices efficiently.

"Field shows nothing but open country below. A few hills, but mostly flat."

"Keep going."

"Still nothing. We're overtaking the terminator."

"Keep going."

The sleek silver yacht shot over the edge of night in to a green dawn, weirdly beautiful, dimmed and pearled by the distortion of the sheltering force-field. The country below was a long tumbling slope that fell from snowcapped mountains across half a continent. Over rocky ledges and tilted plains, to the edge of a tideless sea. It was noontime there, and the glass-green water lay smooth against the shore, and all along the curving edge as far as sight would carry there were ruins, so huge, so wide, and so very old that the meaning of them was lost and they were only a reminder that some mighty thing had been here and now was not.

In an open space that might once have been the greatest starport in the galaxy, hub of an empire that spanned a million stars, one minute speck showed, less than a grain of sand in all that emptiness. Harvey's yacht.

Farah's yacht came down beside it.

There was no sign of life there. The hatch was open. There was no one inside. Everything seemed to be in order, but just inside the hatch, on the metal floor, Lute's sharp eyes saw a fleck of red.

"Blood?"

"It looks like it," Chattan said. He listened to the sultry stillness, and felt cold. "We ought to leave a guard. One of your men, Farah, and one of ours."

Farah nodded. He spoke to one of the men, who returned to Farah's yacht. Chattan said to Doc Brewer, "You, too. Hang onto that gun..." Farah had an arsenal of remarkable completeness aboard and they had armed themselves from it "...and keep alert. We may need help, and you'll be the only man who can give it to us."

He did not add that he was doing his best to live up to the promise he had given Betta.

Doc Brewer made a perfunctory protest, looking uneasily at the wall of tangled forest and humped ruin beyond the ships. Then he too went back to Farah's yacht, obviously relieved.

The others, Farah and his gunman, Chattan and Shemsi and Lute, walked across the broken, buried tarmac and entered the forest, going toward the sea.

A breeze went rustling through the treetops. Down below where the men were there was no breeze. They began to sweat. Their boots stumbled among the ribs of stone and metal left there by dead buildings. Presently they came upon a place where an enormous road had run. The forest was thinner here, held down by the adamantine pavement that defied the trees to root.

There was a path.

It was not much more than a rabbit run, but it had not been made by rabbits, and it was used. Chattan's heart began to beat harder. Small silent shouts of alarm rang through his nervous system.

"Something's alive here, then," he said, and Farah nodded.

Lute, who had been glancing around and sniffing uneasily, said, "Wait while I look ahead." He climbed swiftly into the thicker trees and was gone, agile as any monkey.

The others waited. Twice Chattan thought he heard laughter, but it was so muffled and indistinct that he could not be sure. It sounded like the laughter of children playing hide and seek. Lute came back, scrambling so hurriedly through the branches that he almost fell into Shemsi's arms.

"Up ahead there," he panted. "A dead man. I think he must be one of Harvey's crew." Lute's eyes were wide with horror. "There's something evil here. He...he was tortured to death."

"Did you see anyone?" asked Farah, and Lute said, "No."

They went on, and again Chattan thought he heard the fleeting laughter.

They found the man. What Lute had said was true. The mutilated corpse was hung like a rag doll on a point of metal sticking up through grass and creepers. The point was shaped like a gigantic sword, and perhaps once it had been part of a monument on this triumphal way.

They left it where it was, not knowing what else to do. Lute took to the trees again. They went on, following the path. The salt smell of seawater thickened on the air.

The ancient roadway ended in a vast square, with the whiteness of marble thrusting here and there through the green... marble hands and limbs and noble foreheads, torsos and thighs, scattered like the aftermath of some battle between colossi. At the far side of the square was a building, or rather a part of the walls of what had once been a building, with the green sea showing through them; Even then, roofless and broken as it was, it was staggering to the mind to look at it and recognize its size. And Farah said, in a tone very close to reverence, "That must be the Hall of Suns they speak of in the legends, the real heart and center of the old empire. My God. And I never dreamed it was real."

Lute came down from the high trees and said, "The men we're looking for are there. I saw one of them cross an open space inside."

With their guns ready in their hands, they began to cross the ruined square, between the bits of marble. They were about halfway across when Chattan saw the children.

THERE WERE THREE of them, two boys and a girl, crouched behind a marble head that lay on its side and had only the sad blurred outlines of a face. They sprang up giggling when they knew they had been seen, and Chattan thought that they had deliberately let themselves be discovered. They were quite naked, slender and frail-looking, their skin an indeterminate dun color with a greenish cast. They were marked like Shoba Ruk with a tracery of silver lines, and they looked to be about eight or nine years old, but there was something in their faces that disturbed Chattan, arousing the instinctive revulsion that is caused by something unnatural.

He spoke to them, and they scampered away laughing, peering back over their shoulders with bright secretive eyes. Then they stopped, and the little girl put her finger to her lips and pointed to the walls of the great building. She shook her head and beckoned.

"They want us to follow them," Chattan said.

"Yes, but where? And what are they?" said Farah. "If they're kids, where are their parents? Where do they live? And who killed that poor devil we found on the road back there?"

"I don't know," said Chattan.

Now all three of the children were pantomiming enemies in the great building, enemies lying in wait. They gestured, urging the men to follow in a way they would show them where the enemies would not see.

"They seem friendly enough," Farah said. "They're trying to warn us. Harvey and his men must be waiting for us. They'd have seen us land." He glanced quickly at the gaunt arches of the walls. "We're set-up targets if we go in this way, that's sure. They may know a better one." He made his decision. "It won't hurt to see."

Chattan thought it might very well hurt, but it was only a hunch based on the look in the children's eyes. He followed reluctantly, crouching low, keeping one eye on the ruins. The children ran ahead, laughing.

They passed through a dense screening growth of shrub and vine. And suddenly the children had disappeared and they were in a huge square bay of the walls enclosed on three sides, where a state doorway might once have been. Chattan and Farah both realized the danger even before Lute's cry warned them. The whole party was diving for cover when the first shot was fired, but it was too late for Farah's gunman, who dropped and lay feebly struggling on the ground.

The children had led them with great care into a trap.

Guns fired now from all three sides of the bay. Lying flat in a thicket that grew between the ancient paving stones, Chattan fired back and tried to figure a way out. There didn't seem to be any. They couldn't go back, and they couldn't stay here pinned down. He counted four guns... Harvey, probably Barbour, and VanFleet, one of the crew. Shots were whacking close around him, kicking up dust and chips of stone, searing the leaves of the bushes. Oh hell, he thought, might as well get dropped running as lying still.

"Shemsi," he said. "Lute. Cover me."

He couldn't see them but he knew they were close by, and at once they began blasting the broken walls and window openings with everything they had. Chattan got his feet under him. He broke from the thicket and ran, and hit another clump of brush, rolled under it and out on the other side, and ran again, sideways, on all fours. Inside the walls somebody shouted. Shots came close, so close he could feel the hot breath of their passing, but he couldn't stop now, he was afraid to stop, if he stopped he was dead. He ran and scuttled and rolled, and there was somebody else with him, going low like a big cat with infinite grace and speed. Farah.

They hit the porch together and fell between the mighty sheltering columns and crouched there panting. Footsteps rang on stone inside. Chattan flung one arm across Farah's chest and pressed him back, into the shadowy back of the niche. A man appeared in the doorway, the giant portal from which the doors had ages ago vanished, but which was still magnificent. It was Barbour, edging cautiously around the jamb of carved stone, dwarfed by its height and size. His face was alert and happy. This was his kind of work and he liked it. Chattan let him get all the way through, looking for them, and then he shot him, without any regret.

"Come on," he said to Farah, and they ran together toward the door. Just as they passed through it Chattan looked back into the court. The firing was going on without change, but the children had appeared again. There were two or three others with them now. They had crept out of the woods and caught hold of the wounded man and now they were dragging him back into the woods with them. It dawned on Chattan what had so repelled him about them. Their eyes were not the eyes of children, and they were quite mad. He knew now who had killed the man in the road.

HE HAD NO TIME then to say or do anything about it. Inside the doorway he and Farah took different ways, he to the left, Farah to the right. He crouched and peered around the corner, hearing the firing outside intensify as the three out there prepared to make a rush. Harvey and one of the crewmen were firing through the tall windows. He shouted to them to drop their guns. His voice was drowned in a burst of firing from Farah's side. The crewman spun around and snapped a shot at him, and Chattan dropped him. Harvey stood irresolute, his face white and set, and as crazy in its own way, Chattan thought, as the faces of the maniacal children outside. Farah came running back and said, "There was only one man there. He wasn't as good a shot as he thought he was." His eyes brightened. "Ah," he said. "Harvey."

He raised his gun.

Chattan knocked it down. "Drop it," he said to Harvey. "Drop it while you have the chance."

Harvey dropped it.

The place was quiet now. Shemsi and Lute came in, Shemsi wincing over a flesh-wound in his hip. They all stood around Harvey, and he looked at them like a man who has already died.

Chattan said, "Where is Shoba Ruk?"

Harvey whispered. "Down there."

They turned. And now for the first time Chattan saw the place he had come into, and he forgot everything else for the moment in a rush of awe and wonder.

From this great doorway a double line of columns led for what seemed to the eye an endless distance, across a pavement cumbered now with fallen pediments and the shattered fragments of the roof, but still so long and wide between its enclosing walls that the effect was impressive beyond words. The towering columns supported nothing but the sky, and the green misty sunlight poured in unchecked, and the green ocean showed through the empty window arches. And all across that mighty pavement, under the dust and wreckage, there was a shining and glittering of jewels.

Blazons of empire in the Hall of Suns. Looking out across them, Chattan was stunned...not by the value of the gems which was beyond counting, but by what they stood for. The pavement itself was polished stone as black and deep as space itself, and all across it the suns and constellations burned, the star-colonies, the bright swarming children of this mother-world of men. Here to this place must have come the embassies from Hercules, from Cepheus and Draco and the shining coils of Hydra, from near and far along the brilliant ever-turning star-stream of the Milky Way. Here had been splendor unimaginable, power and pomp beyond belief. Here had been Empire, beside which the greatest empires of Earth were only as candles to a nova.

Then he heard a rustling noise and looked around. The children with the mad eyes had come into the Hall of Suns, laughing as they darted and crept among the ruins, peering at the stranger men.

A cold shook went through Chattan, bringing him sharply back to reality. The mighty Empire had sown its seed through all the galaxy, but it had not endured. Mortal as the puny empires of Egypt and Hatti, it had come crashing down, and now this was left of the mother world, the Heartworld, the cradle of mankind...this wreckage of stone and flesh, cold-shining jewels, cold-shining eyes, empty, all-forgetting, all-forgotten. He looked up at the lethal star that burned above them, and he wondered, and was afraid.

"There he is," said Lute. "I see him. Down there where that covered arch still stands."

Chattan shook himself. He went toward the covered arch by the west wall, and the others came with him, keeping Harvey in the center. And Harvey's feet dragged heavily on the gemmed stars.

Shoba Ruk lay under the arch, bound and gagged. They freed him. He stood up and spoke to them, and Lute and Shemsi looked at him with a queer shyness. This was not the old Lugach they had known so long. This was a man. Chattan had been right. The process of recovery he had seen started on the *Merry Andrew* had been completed during the voyage out with Harvey. Now Shoba Ruk was gaunt and haggard, a man tortured by the possibility of disaster, but mentally whole. He frowned at Chattan, at Shemsi and Lute, as though he only half remembered them, and then he smiled briefly and said, "They were afraid I'd cry out and warn you. Now shall I thank God you're here, or is it only an exchange of evils?"

Farah stepped forward, smiling. "I came here for the treasure, if that's what you mean. Harvey tried to cheat me out of it, but I'm very hard to cheat."

Harvey cursed him in a low harsh whisper. "All my life I've worked and studied and believed. But what are you? A thief."

"You're both thieves," said Shoba Ruk. "Harvey a man possessed, and you... I seem to know you, and I have no good memory as I have of these others."

He looked past Farah at the shadows under the arch, where a vaulted doorway showed, open and unguarded, and from there to the children creeping and tittering among the high columns. Then he looked up, at the green sun.

"So," he said, "you want the treasure of the Heartworld. Shall I tell you what it is? It is death and destruction and madness and horror. It is knowledge, yes. It is power, yes. And its fruits are these."

HIS VOICE RANG against the shattered walls, and the children paused to listen.

"The mother-world grew old, like a human mother. She grew jealous and grasping, and when her children tried to grow and think for themselves she fell into a fury and subdued them with terrible wars, pitting her more obedient sons against rebels. But even that way she could not hold them, and the wars spread and got out of control, and she saw her whole great empire staggering toward collapse, and herself toward ruin. So she isolated herself from the deepening ruin. She poisoned her sun."

He flung up his hand, pointing to the baleful star. "At one and the same time, she rejected her children and protected herself with complete isolation. The force-field allowed life to continue on this planet, but from then on there was no communication with the outside. The parent sun under which life first grew had turned murderous, preventing the mutinous children of the Heartworld from attacking it in force. And the Empire fell, and the Heartworld passed into legend. And here now are the last of your elder brothers, the First Born. Look at them, the fruits of complete isolation, the mad degenerate things who have almost lost the ability to grow up. With each generation fewer and fewer reach maturity. Soon no more will be born at all, and then…"

He made a gesture of finality.

"That is the power Harvey wants. That is the treasure you seek. The knowledge of how to poison a star."

Chattan was speechless with shock. "You mean they did that themselves, deliberately? How?"

"By upsetting the chemical balance of the solar cycle with certain carefully measured charges, so that the radiation output is altered both in kind and intensity. It's all there in the vault, the whole secret, along with others…mostly weapons and destruction, since that was what they specialized in, in the later days. Not one thing beneficial to mankind. I was heartbroken when I first entered it, to find nothing there but death."

Harvey's eyes blazed with dull fire. "It's not for you to judge. You're a scholar, not a scientist."

"And I'm a thief." said Farah softly. "Good enough. This is the greatest hoard in the galaxy, and there's no telling the price it'll bring. I'll take it."

Chattan said, "No."

Farah looked at him and laughed, and raised a gun. Chattan dived in low, the gun-blast searing his shoulder. He groped for the weapon and couldn't get hold of it.

Then, suddenly, right in front of his eyes, Farah's face went purple as two great hands gripped his throat from behind. They were Shemsi's hands, and Shemsi shook Farah once, not gently, and the gun fell from his hand.

The children tittered and drew near.

"Bind him," said Shoba Ruk, looking at Farah. "I am going now to do what I should have done before. I was afraid to take the responsibility then. Now I know I must. I am going to destroy the vault."

"No," cried Harvey. "No, no. Stop him."

He ran suddenly and placed himself between Shoba Ruk and the open door of the vault.

Shoba Ruk shook his head. "You haven't the key, Harvey. I told you that. You can't enter without the key. And I have it." He touched the silver markings on his skin.

Chattan stared, unbelievingly. "You mean...the tattooing on your body is the key?"

Shoba Ruk nodded. "Yes. A metallic pattern, always the same, that lets a man who wears it on his skin pass through the gateway without triggering the forces that guard it." He looked at the tittering children. *"They* have the key upon them, just as their forefathers long ago had it, a pattern coming unchanged down through the ages. I made friends with these little ones and they put the key-pattern on my skin. They did it gladly...it is very painful, and they enjoy pain. They killed the others, all but two..."

He stopped, and then said, "It is the talisman, with which the men of the Heartworld guarded their most secret vault. And without it you can't go in, Harvey. Never."

Harvey whispered, "I don't believe you. It's a lie to frighten me away. I won't let you destroy it. It's mine, and the Heartworld is mine. All these years... There are weapons in there. I'll stop you."

He turned and plunged through the door of the vault.

Instantly there was a flare of white light so intense that Chattan was blinded by it even at that distance. For a fraction of a second Harvey was caught motionless in the center of it, and then he was gone. Literally gone, leaving no trace. They stood, staring, dazed and stunned by the brief and terrible violence of that end.

There was a moment of silence, and then, quite steadily, his head erect, Shoba Ruk went through the doorway into the vault.

HOURS LATER, Farah's yacht, approached the final stage of its dangerous journey back along the eclipse-shadow path.

Farah, much subdued, was at the controls with Chattan. Doc Brewer, with Shemsi and Lute beside him, sat very quietly, sweating out the passage, and glancing covertly from time to time at Shoba Ruk, who had returned to his old pose of brooding. Behind them, the Heartworld was only a dark disc against the deadly sun.

"So much power," said Shoba Ruk, hardly realizing that he spoke. "I had it in my hands, and I let it go. I let it go."

Chattan realized that Shoba Ruk was human, too, and tempted by the same things that tempted others.

"You did the right thing," he said, looking at the evil green light outside their path of darkness. "No man, no world, should have that secret!"

He glanced at Farah, but the master-thief kept his head averted.

The yacht emerged from the shadow, beyond the danger point.

Chattan looked at free space, blazing with its loops and chains and rivers of stars, the beautiful domain of man given to him by the mother-world in the days of her youth. That glory she had had, that good she had done. Let her memory rest in peace.

The yacht slipped into overdrive, on the way back to Algol One and a girl named Betta.

THE END

If you've enjoyed this book, you will not want to miss these terrific titles…

ARMCHAIR SCI-FI & HORROR DOUBLE NOVELS, $12.95 each

D-171 **REGAN'S PLANET** by Robert Silverberg
SOMEONE TO WATCH OVER ME by H. L. Gold and Floyd Gale

D-172 **PEOPLE MINUS X** by Raymond Z. Gallun
THE SAVAGE MACHINE by Randall Garrett

D-173 **THE FACE BEYOND THE VEIL** by Rog Phillips
REST IN AGONY by Paul W. Fairman

D-174 **VIRGIN OF VALKARION** by Poul Anderson
EARTH ALERT by Kris Neville

D-175 **WHEN THE ATOMS FAILED** by John W. Campbell, Jr.
DRAGONS OF SPACE by Aladra Septama

D-176 **THE TATTOOED MAN** by Edmond Hamilton
A RESCUE FROM JUPITER by Gawain Edwards

D-177 **THE FLYING THREAT** by David H. Keller, M. D.
THE FIFTH-DIMENSION TUBE by Murray Leinster

D-178 **LAST DAYS OF THRONAS** by S. J. Byrne
GODDESS OF WORLD 21 by Henry Slesar

D-179 **THE MOTHER WORLD** by B. Wallis & George C. Wallis
BEYOND THE VANISHING POINT by Ray Cummings

D-180 **DARK DESTINY** by Dwight V. Swain
SECRET OF PLANETOID 88 by Ed Earl Repp

ARMCHAIR SCIENCE FICTION CLASSICS, $12.95 each

C-69 **EXILES OF THE MOON**
by Nathan Schachner & Arthur Leo Zagut

C-70 **SKYLARK OF SPACE**
by E. E. "Doc' Smith

ARMCHAIR MYSTERY-CRIME DOUBLE NOVELS, $12.95 each

B-11 **THE BABY DOLL MURDERS** by James O. Causey
DEATH HITCHES A RIDE by Martin L. Weiss

B-12 **THE DOVE** by Milton Ozaki
THE GLASS LADDER by Paul W. Fairman

B-13 **THE NAKED STORM** by C. M. Kornbluth
THE MAN OUTSIDE by Alexander Blade

If you've enjoyed this book, you will not want to miss these terrific titles…

ARMCHAIR SCI-FI & HORROR DOUBLE NOVELS, $12.95 each

D-51 **A GOD NAMED SMITH** by Henry Slesar
 WORLDS OF THE IMPERIUM by Keith Laumer

D-52 **CRAIG'S BOOK** by Don Wilcox
 EDGE OF THE KNIFE by H. Beam Piper

D-53 **THE SHINING CITY** by Rena M. Vale
 THE RED PLANET by Russ Winterbotham

D-54 **THE MAN WHO LIVED TWICE** by Rog Phillips
 VALLEY OF THE CROEN by Lee Tarbell

D-55 **OPERATION DISASTER** by Milton Lesser
 LAND OF THE DAMNED by Berkeley Livingston

D-56 **CAPTIVE OF THE CENTAURIANESS** by Poul Anderson
 A PRINCESS OF MARS by Edgar Rice Burroughs

D-57 **THE NON-STATISTICAL MAN** by Raymond F. Jones
 MISSION FROM MARS by Rick Conroy

D-58 **INTRUDERS FROM THE STARS** by Ross Rocklynne
 FLIGHT OF THE STARLING by Chester S. Geier

D-59 **COSMIC SABOTEUR** by Frank M. Robinson
 LOOK TO THE STARS by Willard Hawkins

D-60 **THE MOON IS HELL!** by John W. Campbell, Jr.
 THE GREEN WORLD by Hal Clement

ARMCHAIR SCIENCE FICTION CLASSICS, $12.95 each

C-16 **THE SHAVER MYSTERY, Book Three**
 by Richard S. Shaver

C-17 **THE PLANET STRAPPERS**
 by Raymond Z. Gallun

C-18 **THE FOURTH "R"**
 by George O. Smith

ARMCHAIR SCI-FI & HORROR GEMS SERIES, $12.95 each

G-5 **SCIENCE FICTION GEMS, Vol. Three**
 C. M. Kornbluth and others

G-6 **HORROR GEMS, Vol. Three**
 August Derleth and others

If you've enjoyed this book, you will not want to miss these terrific titles...

ARMCHAIR SCI-FI & HORROR DOUBLE NOVELS, $12.95 each

D-61 **THE MAN WHO STOPPED AT NOTHING** by Paul W. Fairman
TEN FROM INFINITY by Ivar Jorgensen

D-62 **WORLDS WITHIN** by Rog Phillips
THE SLAVE by C.M. Kornbluth

D-63 **SECRET OF THE BLACK PLANET** by Milton Lesser
THE OUTCASTS OF SOLAR III by Emmett McDowell

D-64 **WEB OF THE WORLDS** by Harry Harrison and Katherine MacLean
RULE GOLDEN by Damon Knight

D-65 **TEN TO THE STARS** by Raymond Z. Gallun
THE CONQUERORS by David H. Keller, M. D.

D-66 **THE HORDE FROM INFINITY** by Dwight V. Swain
THE DAY THE EARTH FROZE by Gerald Hatch

D-67 **THE WAR OF THE WORLDS** by H. G. Wells
THE TIME MACHINE by H. G. Wells

D-68 **STARCOMBERS** by Edmond Hamilton
THE YEAR WHEN STARDUST FELL by Raymond F. Jones

D-69 **HOCUS-POCUS UNIVERSE** by Jack Williamson
QUEEN OF THE PANTHER WORLD by Berkeley Livingston

D-70 **BATTERING RAMS OF SPACE** by Don Wilcox
DOOMSDAY WING by George H. Smith

ARMCHAIR SCIENCE FICTION CLASSICS, $12.95 each

C-19 **EMPIRE OF JEGGA**
by David V. Reed

C-20 **THE TOMORROW PEOPLE**
by Judith Merrll

C-21 **THE MAN FROM YESTERDAY**
by Howard Browne as by Lee Francis

C-22 **THE TIME TRADERS**
by Andre Norton

C-23 **ISLANDS OF SPACE**
by John W. Campbell

C-24 **THE GALAXY PRIMES**
by E. E. "Doc" Smith

If you've enjoyed this book, you will not want to miss these terrific titles…

ARMCHAIR SCI-FI & HORROR DOUBLE NOVELS, $12.95 each

ARMCHAIR SCIENCE FICTION CLASSICS, $12.95 each

ARMCHAIR SCI-FI & HORROR GEMS SERIES, $12.95 each

If you've enjoyed this book, you will not want to miss these terrific titles…

ARMCHAIR SCI-FI & HORROR DOUBLE NOVELS, $12.95 each

D-81   **THE LAST PLEA** by Robert Bloch
       OMEGA by Robert Sheckley

D-82   **WOMAN FROM ANOTHER PLANET** by Frank Belknap Long
       HOMECALLING by Judith Merril

D-83   **WHEN TWO WORLDS MEET** by Robert Moore Williams
       THE MAN WHO HAD NO BRAINS by Jeff Sutton

D-84   **THE SPECTRE OF SUICIDE SWAMP** by E. K. Jarvis
       IT'S MAGIC, YOU DOPE! by Jack Sharkey

D-85   **THE STARSHIP FROM SIRIUS** by Rog Phillips
       THE FINAL WEAPON by Everett Cole

D-86   **TREASURE ON THUNDER MOON** by Edmond Hamilton
       TRAIL OF THE ASTROGAR by Henry Hasse

D-87   **THE VENUS ENIGMA** by Joe Gibson
       THE WOMAN IN SKIN 13 by Paul W. Fairman

D-88   **THE MAD ROBOT** by William P. McGivern
       THE RUNNING MAN by J. Holly Hunter

D-89   **VENGEANCE OF KYVOR** by Randall Garrett
       AT THE EARTH'S CORE by Edgar Rice Burroughs

D-90   **DWELLERS OF THE DEEP** by Don Wilcox
       NIGHT OF THE LONG KNIVES by Fritz Leiber

ARMCHAIR SCIENCE FICTION CLASSICS, $12.95 each

C-28   **THE MAN FROM TOMORROW**
       by Stanton A. Coblentz

C-29   **THE GREEN MAN OF GRAYPEC**
       by Festus Pragnell

C-30   **THE SHAVER MYSTERY, Book Four**
       by Richard S. Shaver

ARMCHAIR MASTERS OF SCIENCE FICTION SERIES, $16.95 each

MS-7   **MASTERS OF SCIENCE FICTION AND FANTASY, Vol. Seven**
       Lester del Rey, "The Band Played On" and other tales

MS-8   **MASTERS OF SCIENCE FICTION, Vol. Eight**
       Milton Lesser, "'A' is for Android" and other tales

If you've enjoyed this book, you will not want to miss these terrific titles...

ARMCHAIR SCI-FI & HORROR DOUBLE NOVELS, $12.95 each

D-91 **THE TIME TRAP** by Henry Kuttner
THE LUNAR LICHEN by Hal Clement

D-92 **SARGASSO OF LOST STARSHIPS** by Poul Anderson
THE ICE QUEEN by Don Wilcox

D-93 **THE PRINCE OF SPACE** by Jack Williamson
POWER by Harl Vincent

D-94 **PLANET OF NO RETURN** by Howard Browne
THE ANNIHILATOR COMES by Ed Earl Repp

D-95 **THE SINISTER INVASION** by Edmond Hamilton
OPERATION TERROR by Murray Leinster

D-96 **TRANSIENT** by Ward Moore
THE WORLD-MOVER by George O. Smith

D-97 **FORTY DAYS HAS SEPTEMBER** by Milton Lesser
THE DEVIL'S PLANET by David Wright O'Brien

D-98 **THE CYBERENE** by Rog Phillips
BADGE OF INFAMY by Lester del Rey

D-99 **THE JUSTICE OF MARTIN BRAND** by Raymond A. Palmer
BRING BACK MY BRAIN by Dwight V. Swain

D-100 **WIDE-OPEN PLANET** by L. Sprague de Camp
AND THEN THE TOWN TOOK OFF by Richard Wilson

ARMCHAIR SCIENCE FICTION CLASSICS, $12.95 each

C-31 **THE GOLDEN GUARDSMEN**
by S. J. Byrne

C-32 **ONE AGAINST THE MOON**
by Donald A. Wollheim

C-33 **HIDDEN CITY**
by Chester S. Geier

ARMCHAIR SCI-FI & HORROR GEMS SERIES, $12.95 each

G-9 **SCIENCE FICTION GEMS, Vol. Five**
Clifford D. Simak and others

G-10 **HORROR GEMS, Vol. Five**
E. Hoffmann Price and others

A RACE DOOMED TO EXTINCTION...?

When an expedition from Jupiter lands on Tellus, they find the planet entirely without water and no apparent life. However, Allus Marce, a member of the team, finds the remains of a vast city. Towering above it all is a strange statue of a man clutching a cylinder. Scientifically curious, Marce takes the cylinder and is surprised to find a strange message sealed within…

Meanwhile, beneath the statue lays a great cavern with a large underground lake. There, an old man has survived with his daughter and son, the last remnants of the human race on Tellus. Their only hope of survival is for someone to find their plea for help, which is now in the hands of Allus Marce on the surface far above. That message is not only a plea for their survival, but for the survival of mankind itself…

CAST OF CHARACTERS

ALLUS MARCE
This young adventurer wanted to sow his oats a while longer, before he took his fathers place to lead a revolution.

SALVARIUS CARDE
A brutal and selfish man of extreme military prowess, whose only interest lay in his desire for glory—at the expense of other men.

NINA
Being the last woman on Earth, she was obviously a key component to the survival of the human race.

OLD MAN
It was his hope that the human race could survive. Unfortunately the odds weren't in their favor—and death was soon at their door.

EMPEROR DOLMICIAN
Brimming with confidence, this megalomaniac was convinced of his absolute power and greatness over his beleaguered subjects.

NINO
A hard worker whose goal was to display a message in the "statue," with hopes of a rescue from somewhere—anywhere.

A RESCUE
FROM JUPITER

By
GAWAIN EDWARDS

ARMCHAIR FICTION
PO Box 4369, Medford, Oregon 97504

*For more information about Armchair Books and products, visit our
website at...*

www.armchairfiction.com

Or email us at...

armchairfiction@yahoo.com

CHAPTER ONE

WHEN the first explorers from the planet Jupiter, which they called Pleida reached the planet Tellus (which its former inhabitants had called Earth) they found there little to recommend it. Even at the first glance, it was obvious that Tellus was no longer habitable; if indeed it had ever known a race of intelligent beings. In the enormous open areas, which formerly were supposed to be covered with water, only tremendous dry fields of salt were found. Even at the poles, where enduring icecaps had once lain, there remained almost no moisture. Upon the arid backs of the former continents there was none; not even traces of former desert life could be seen. The Earth was a sorry remnant of a world, unhappily dead before its time—a dry rock, wearily wheeling its age-old way around the sun.

The leader of the expedition from Pleida, Salvarius Carde, had found the journey to Tellus a long and dangerous one; and he did not desire to return without some definite proof, whether or not there had once been sentient life on the planet. Throughout the infancy of his own race, there had been a well-defined belief that intelligent beings, for many generations, had inhabited Tellus; there was, in fact, a Pleidan myth that people from Tellus had once visited Pleida in a protracted search for land suitable to human life. Though the surface indications of Tellus seemed to belie any tradition of life's having existed here. Salvarius Carde had ordered the eighty-nine men engaged with him in the exploration of the planet to scatter widely over its surface and to learn, if possible, whether there ever had been any inhabitants; and, if so, to seek also what had become of them.

Thereafter, for a third of the smaller planet's year, the envoys from Pleida had searched the surface of Tellus, their great white wings carrying them quickly here and there. The

A Rescue from Jupiter

by
Gawain Edwards

"Then, while I poised there, the figure dropped its arm and, quick as a plummet, dropped through an opening and disappeared. I tried to leap forward and catch it; but the automatic mechanism was too quick."

brilliant sun reflected from the mountains and deserts seamed with crystal salt, hurt their eyes; thirst turned them back again and again to their spaceship for new supplies of water. The seemingly utter uselessness of the quest caused many to urge repeatedly that it be given up; but Salvarius was a man of iron. He commanded them to cover all the planet; to miss not the least portion of its area and to report all that they found.

It was only after many days had passed, at the time of year when the northern pole of Tellus tilts away from the sun that Allus Marce, the most vigorous of the explorers, returned to the spaceship bearing in his strong hands a metallic cylinder of a dull color, evidently worn by the elements.

"I have found traces of the abode of man," he declared. "They are at the very bottom of what was once an ocean. Dying for want of water, these humans followed the receding moisture to the lowest place on the face of Tellus; and when the water disappeared, so did they. It was there I found this cylinder, which may contain writings; perhaps a history of this strange race."

"Were there other relics?" his captain asked.

"Many evidences of a once great civilization; traces of engines, long since oxidized away; stone walls still standing amid the dunes, glittering with crystalline salt like the endless hills."

"But no living beings?"

"None that I observed. There are no traces of cultivation; no water is left in the great salt lake that once lay in the hollow. I could not see how life could have continued to exist there."

"Tell me the circumstances of the finding of this cylinder; and why you believe it contains writings, though none appear on the surface of it."

Marce's Story

ALLUS MARCE hesitated for breath before he replied. Then, facing his superior, he recounted how his search, conscientiously carried out, had taken him over illimitable deserts—waterless, and lifeless, without even the shifting caused by great winds to change the monotony of the landscape. At length, he had come abruptly upon a valley miles in length, and of a depth which marked it immediately as the lowest spot on the surface of the planet. It was in the southern hemisphere, he explained, near the middle of what had once been the largest ocean of Tellus.

"Perceiving that I had here found a portion of the planet never before visited by men from our own world," he continued, "I entered into it cautiously, moving slowly, close to the surface of the ground, my eyes seeking continually for any trace of those lost man-beings which our lore tells us once existed here. The floor of this valley had once been level sea-bottom, and its walls were rocky cliffs, descending deep into the Earth. But, as the water of the ocean had dried up, vast deposits of salt, deeper and of a clearer substance than any I had seen elsewhere on the globe, had covered the surface with a white and crystalline coat, reflecting the sun from countless facets until my eyes could hardly stand the glare. It was like entering a valley strewn with layers of the finest cut jewels. The sun's rays were reflected; multiplied, it seemed, a thousand-fold. And everywhere was eternal sterility. The deposits of crystal salts had fallen upon the steep-cut sides, like talus at the footing of a weathered cliff. At different levels, down the sides, were giant ledges of lime and salt as if, at each of these succeeding levels, the water had stood for many years, creating shoreline after shoreline, each lower than the last; until at last the life-giving moisture went up into the dry air, and left old Tellus arid."

"Yes—" broke in Salvarius with impatience, "but the cylinder, and the traces of the dying race—?"

The younger man was firm in his desire to tell his story in his own way. "These details are important," he asserted, "if you are to understand the last wretched struggle of this people at the bottom of what had once been this world's deepest sea. For it was at that deep-deft valley, I am sure, that the final drama was enacted."

"Go on," this from Salvarius.

"I came, at length, examining ledge after ledge, down the steepest side to the bottom of the valley, which is broad and level, and of a length, I should say, about one three-hundred-sixtieth of the polar diameter of the planet. Its axis lay, roughly, at an angle midway between the line of the equator and a line drawn directly from pole to pole. The deposit of earth in the bottom was deep and thoroughly intermingled with crystallized salt; but here and there outcrops of rock jutted through. The lowest portion of this bottom was near the center of the valley; and toward this basin, indicated broadly to the eye by the contour of the layers of deposited salt, I carefully made my flight.

"I had not gone far before I began to perceive that what I had formerly thought to be natural rocky projections, reaching upward through the soil, were really the outlines of a once-formidable city of stone. The work of the hand of man, upon the uppermost sides of the blocks that met my eye, was unmistakable. Pausing, I cast my eye back over the valley floor whence I had come. I then saw that, at some time in the distant past, this whole area had been covered with stone buildings arranged in geometrical rows, with streets between, and squares, courts, avenues, and open ways.

"Like some avenging power, the shifting soil, which once had formed at the bottom of an endless sea, had drifted with the brief eddying winds, which still linger here into the outer fringes of that city. With the passage of time, new deposits had been blown into the gulf, to further obliterate the work of men. I know not whether there were men still living there when the dunes first came. I could not tell whether the last weak members of the race, caught between the drought on one hand and the encroaching dust storms on the other, had lived to see their last stronghold on the Earth buried before their eyes; or whether, mercifully, they were all dead and gone before the burial began.

"In any case, perceiving that the hummocks of stone over which I had been flying were not natural pillars of living rock, but rather the tops and spires of an extinct city, I hovered carefully among them; always directing my progress toward the lowest part of the vale, where the last remnant of all the water of Tellus had once lain. As I proceeded, I reached an area where the drifting dust has not yet completed its work; the upper parts of buildings project here above the surface. Cemented by hands now dead, great slabs of stone lie roof-like upon pillars cut and curiously carved.

"Still I proceeded on. Now, as I moved, I found myself above what had once been a street, though covered probably by a hundred feet of Earth. On either side the buildings rise; some tall and stately, reminiscent of wealth and refinement; others less attractive, but fascinating still for the story they could tell. Here and there a tall-spired building thrusts its finger of stone high into the air above the sand. These places I took to be temples for ceremonials of some kind.

The Cylinder

"ABRUPTLY, as I glided, the city seemed to fall away and end on the shoreline of what was once a vast and ancient lake. There still may be seen the crusted ledge which indicates the former water level at the bases of these stately buildings. Beyond it, the basin dips to deeper levels, and here also are the successive water-line's, which marked the agonies of a despairing city. Strewn far and near amid the cruel salt, I perceived what might once have been bones; but whether of man or beast I could not say. Were they the wretches who had lived to see the final remnant of water vanishing—what scenes had been enacted in this basin?

"It was at this point, when I was about to turn back to search among the ruins for some tangible evidence of human life to bring to you, that I beheld far off, rising above the very lowest spot of all the vast salt basin where I hovered, a mighty tower of stone, rounded and firm, projecting upwards some hundreds of feet. How it had come that I had previously overlooked it I cannot tell, unless it was from the blinding glare of sun on salt.

"I cannot tell you with what mingled feelings of dread, hope and curiosity I beheld this last upright relic of a vanished race. As if by instinct I knew it for what it is—a mighty tombstone erected by the last survivors of the men on Earth to commemorate all who had died, and to remain throughout the ages as proof that the race had lived.

"Perceiving that the drift would ultimately fill their wide streets with its glittering substance, and in time the mighty city itself would be buried beneath the desert these people must have selected the spot where their last remnant of water was collected, to erect this mighty monument. They made it high enough to escape indefinitely the encroachment of the sand—firm enough to last eternities, and beautiful enough to attest to the art and science of a forgotten race.

"Straight up it rises like some huge crystal of milky quartz, fashioned of a substance I have never seen before; seamless and bright and of such proportions as to take the breath away. Its base had been planted in the Earth to an unknown depth. It is as broad and wide where it emerges from the surface as the highest building in Nealoma, our foremost city on Pleida. In rising upward it slopes inward on every side to form curving terraces, so contrived as to excite the mind and cause the eye to sweep on upward to the heights.

"I passed around it just above the ground and found no door or opening of any kind. The glassy surface reflected the sun as sharply as the innumerable glittering crystals of salt, which lay on every side. I perceived that it is, indeed, at the lowest spot in the whole valley, the spot where the last remnant of Earth's last lake had been. The sand has not yet drifted there; in fact the Earth, it seemed to me, has hardly dried. We did not come very much too late. O Salvarius Carde, to find some moisture on the Earth. Perhaps five Earthly years ago, perhaps but one or two, there was a little pool of salty water standing there. It is clear that the tower was built *before the water was all gone.* There are no tracks about the base of the tower; there are no signs of skeletons for hundreds of yards. It seemed as if the Tellurian people, perceiving that their end was near and inevitable, had built up their cenotaph, buried their dead, and themselves committed suicide rather than undergo the tortures of death by thirst and hunger."

"But the cylinder—" interposed Salvarius Carde, put out by so much explanation and detail.

"Ah, yes, the cylinder," Marce replied. "I will come to that at once."

He cleared his throat, speaking louder so that other members of the expedition might hear him.

"As I moved around the tower and found no door, it occurred to me that these Tellurian engineers had refrained from leaving an opening near the base of their shaft for the obvious reason that the drift would soon reach it and close if up. For the same reason, they had left no writings near the base. One should look for these things nearer the top, perhaps upon the top itself.

"Deciding that this reasoning was accurate, I rose higher into the air and circled the tall shaft upward, moving around and around, my eyes upon the polished surfaces gleaming in the sun. There are no marks, no inscriptions, no doors or windows, no signs of any kind on any side. Upward I swept, until at length I beheld that the top is not flat, but slopes broadly like the ends of certain crystals. Here, there is neither a door, nor inscription; but before my startled eyes there stood a single figure, carved of the same glittering stuff as the tower itself, and shaped, I take it, like the members of the race that had left it there.

Back To Pleida!

"THERE is this difference, however, between the material of the figure and that of the tower. Whereas the substance that formed the building is almost white, milky-clear and highly polished, this startling figure standing silently at the top was *black*. It was the statue, I presume, of a Tellurian man, perhaps a priest or scientist. There was no beard; the garments were loose and flowing and fell below the knees. An object rested upon the head, perhaps a badge of distinction, and the left hand clasped a rod, the end of which rested on the pedestal. It seemed obviously a staff of authority or a symbol of some custom.

"But what interested me most was that in the right hand out-thrust in the gesture of bestowing a gift, was this cylinder. Upon the face of the figure there seemed to be a sad and weary smile, as if upon the completion of the mission in which he was engaged, he, too, would die and disappear. The figure appeared to be fast and firm at the base, as though melted into the substance upon which it stood.

"Since the outstretched hand clearly invited the beholder to take the cylinder, I alighted, and, sought to do so; but at first I could see no way to loosen the stony grasp and wrench it free.

"It seemed uncouth and ghoulish to grapple with that stone replica of a dead race, even upon invitation to wrest from its grasp the object it had held so long. But, at last, I beheld that the thumb of the outstretched hand, which closed over the top of the cylinder, was so contrived that with a little lateral pressure it could be moved aside. Quickly I did this, and was then able to pull the cylinder away. The thumb moved back into place, as if actuated by a hidden spring. *And, though I may be thought insane when I declare it, I heard the image sigh, as in relief.*

"Then, while I poised there, amazed, inarticulate with surprise and horror, the surface beneath the statue automatically moved, turning half around to the accompaniment of a humming sound. The figure slowly dropped its arm. Its face, turned toward me still, bent on me that sad, inscrutable smile; and quick as a plummet, the whole figure dropped through an opening and disappeared. I tried to leap forward and catch it; but the automatic mechanism, which had undoubtedly removed the thing, was too quick for me. There was a loud snap; and a trapdoor had closed the opening so tightly that no efforts of mine could budge it.

"Atop the crystal tower, now bare, I stood with the ancient cylinder in my trembling hands.

"I spread my wings and brought it here to you, as swiftly as I could pass through the Tellurian air."

Allus Marce bowed his head while Salvarius Carde stared at him. The leader regarded the cylinder with new interest, as though speculating on the truth of the younger man's story.

"It is enough," he said; "Allus Marce, you shall be rewarded for bringing this—provided it contains the evidence we are looking for."

Mechanics were summoned; in the presence of all the members of the expedition, they twisted open the metal case. Inside were many sheets, closely written, in a script none among them could interpret.

"I should like to stay and investigate further," said Salvarius at length, "but already we have overstayed our time. Our supplies have run short and the only useful element this planet can give us is oxygen. We will take for granted that this message can be deciphered on Pleida by our scholars, and that it will tell us all we care to know."

He called the explorers in, the mechanics and engineers, the space navigators and the rocket experts. With their help, he refilled his tanks with oxygen for the return journey. Some of the men took stones from Tellus to commemorate their exploit; others preferred to have about them no object to remind them of the dreary days on this scarred and lifeless planet.

The mighty doors of the space flier were closed and made fast. The rockets suddenly roared, and the ship flew upward like a brilliant bird a-wing, straight toward the sun; then turning, it moved off in the direction of Pleida.

CHAPTER TWO
The Wailing Cry

THE burning disc of the sun had passed once more over the parched plains of the dying world; it was near its setting beyond the deep valley that Allus Marce had visited. The last harsh rays played brightly upon the fields of salt; turning them to gold and crimson upon the heights until the valley seemed filled with blood. The sun's beams, passing through the millions of miles of cold outer space as with a purpose foreordained, reached across the farthest heights of the valley's edge and touched with a delicate yellow finger the upper part of the milky shaft. Thus outlined, it stood like a sentinel guarding the basin, below the ruined city and its dead.

Everywhere lay the encroaching drifts, the gleaming salt. The tower itself, a finger of almost luminous beauty, betokening the spirit and strength of a race now vanished, seemed alone among the works of man to have survived. It alone had defeated the forces of destruction, which were concentrating their efforts here to wipe out the last of human handiwork. Of the buildings of the ruined city, only a few at the very fringe of the lowest basin were still standing; and already they were leaning crazily this way and that, groaning with the weight of years.

Even as the sun settled westward at the valley's amber rim, one of the few remaining edifices of brick and stone gave up its brave struggle against the drift. With a rumbling sound, which travelled up the barren valley and echoed back, it fell outward into the dry bed of the ancient lake. Clouds of white dust, released from the mortar and stone, rolled upward in the still evening air.

Was it an illusion that at that moment, as eternal silence settled once again upon the valley, a thin, wailing cry arose from the ruins of the demolished building?

Following hard upon the mighty rumble, which had marked the building's end, the valley was suddenly tremulous with a cry, half human, half animal, at first rising in pain and despair, then quieting to resignation. Then it ended in a strangling sound. If it were a man who uttered such a sound, then his cry was that of all the race that had gone down to death, suffering from the consequences of its own sins. It was the cry as well of plants and animals, of worms and slimy things, of bird and beast and reptile from the beginning of living time; it was the universal wail of despair and then of resignation in the face of death.

The thin echoes rolled against the precipitous valley walls, and echoed back again. Then came silence. Not even the common rustles of the night, birds or insects, marauding beasts, or fluttering bats were there to voice their presence in the fast-approaching night. The end of the world and the universe, would not find old Tellus more deathly still than it was then.

The smothering dust settled slowly back. The cries from beneath the debris had ceased. No eye upon the surface of all that hollow could have discerned the slightest sign or hint of life. It seemed, indeed, that the world was dead.

Never the less, there was life on Tellus still. The milky tower, now glistening in the twilight like a fountain of silver, ran like a hollow needle far into the Earth beneath. There, at its lower end, a passageway led northward. Beneath the valley's boundary cliffs it passed and onward toward the north beneath dry mountains of ledged and furrowed rock.

For a distance greater than half a mile it passed that way. Then, with a quick turn, it rounded a glittering adamantine substance in its path and opened suddenly upon a subterranean chamber so vast, so hollow and alive with echoes, so bright with phosphorescence and the sparkle of light from many-faceted jewels, that the first man who beheld it must have stood amazed.

Waiting

IT was one of those underground hollows long known to exist beneath the Earth, hollows lighted by a natural radiance and supporting forms of life of its own. This one, like many another of lesser extent had in its center a cool, silent lake of the purest water. Within the deeps moved fish of strange kind, such as had never been seen on the surface. Upon the murky shores there were many varieties of pulpy plants, evil and unhealthy to look upon, but nevertheless alive.

The gloomy lake was perhaps a mile long, and somewhat more than half as broad. The sloping beaches moved away fanwise on every side, until they touched the serried cliffs that formed the cavern's walls. The roof was domed and fantastically carved; as though the hand of a playful giant, having at his command every gem and metal, had amused himself with tracing patterns and arrangements intricate beyond human comprehension. Perhaps pleased with his handiwork, he had placed behind it a chemical luminescence, which brought out the details like a cameo; a jewel framed in the everlasting rock!

Along the left bank, skirting the silent edges of the pool, a footpath ran from the mouth of the passageway to a point almost at the opposite end of the cavern. Here a series of low, dark spots betrayed the openings of cavern-chains beyond. In the centermost of these openings glowed a faint yellow flickering light of fragile warmth. Against its glow, from time to time, there appeared, in the opening, the shadowy form of a human being, clad in loose-fitting robes.

As it passed the portal it often paused, as if to survey the lake, the beach, and the strange vegetation. It was, plainly, watching for the approach of someone from the direction of the passageway that led toward the milky tower and the city's ruins.

But no such person approached. There was nothing to be seen but the quiet pool, the never-moving fronds of the vegetation and the flicker of the light above as it played upon the jeweled dome.

The interior of the great chamber, for all its brightness and display, was intensely quiet, more silent if possible than the dead world outside. The slimy creatures of the water's depths never broke splashingly to the surface but crept along the bottom, burrowing in the mud. Among the patches where vegetation grew, there were other living creatures; but they, too, moved silently here and there, as though the oppression of the centuries were upon them—as if they dared not break the silence, which had lain upon that air so long.

Thus it was that the sound of human voices came drifting at frequent intervals across the pool. There was a heavy voice, and another that answered it in lighter tones.

"He isn't coming yet?" the deep voice inquired. "He's not in sight."

"Then something has happened. Something unusual has kept him out. He's never been so late before."

"But what *could* happen?" the softer voice replied in alarm. "It has been centuries since there were animals. We have no enemies..." The voice laughed bitterly: "...He has only stopped outside longer than there was need, perhaps to watch the sky. It's bright and cool these nights; there are no clouds—"

Then, later, the deep voice said:

"I wish you'd go and see."

The shadowy figure came to the portal once more, and stood there, staring out into the greater cavern for some time. At length it turned back again.

"I'm worried," confessed the heavier voice again. "There's bitter irony in that, too. Imagine, trying to maintain the last spark of human life on a dead planet. Imagine, when we are all doomed to death and extinction with the passing of your life, his and my own, that we should struggle for the prolongation, even by a day, of our wretched existences!"

The same figure reappeared in the entrance suddenly. With some remark that was swallowed up in the depths of the cave behind, it advanced rapidly along the path toward the outer passageway. The figure was slight and quick; yet in the manner of walking it betrayed a certain resilient strength and endurance.

As it drew near the entrance to the passage, the light fell upon it more fully from above; and it was plain that the slender figure was that of a young woman—hardly more than a girl—with a body so beautifully formed that its lines showed their splendor, despite the concealment of the flowing wrap about her. Her face was finely cut, the features regular and strong, the eyes bright and intelligent. Her mouth was sensitive and delicate; but it also showed determination of purpose and fortitude; qualities that were needed, surely, for an existence such as this!

But there was about her something more striking than any of these things. As though carefully tinted by a most exquisite artistry, her skin was a deep, ebony black. Supple and firm.

In her right hand she carried a flaming torch, though it was scarcely needed in the brightness of the cavern. The smoke from it whirled up overhead as she walked. The flame, moving first to one side and then to the other, by turns illuminated her face and obscured it. The torch, the trail of smoke, and the shrouded ebon figure moving quickly along the narrow, well-worn pathway beside the motionless lake were like the figments of a haunted dream.

She walked quickly, with a firm, even tread—unafraid, yet with evident distaste for the gloom and strangeness about her. When she reached the opalescent boulder, around the left side of which the passage ran outward toward the tower, she paused for a moment, while the flame above her head blazed high.

"Nino! Nino!" she called.

The echoes answered her, howling like demons from the vaulted roof, the dripping walls, the bosom of the deep lake. There was no other sound.

Pausing for another moment as if undecided, she finally turned her back upon the opening at the left of the obstruction and passed partly around it. She entered a smaller passage at the right, which ran outward, beneath the valley, in a somewhat different direction. She was now walking toward the city, which the drifting dunes had stolen from its builders.

The yellow reflection from the torch followed her for a moment down the passageway, and was gone.

CHAPTER THREE
His Kingdom

THE light of the open fire flickered uncertainly, in the rocky inner cave, sending its yellow rays against the rough-hewn walls where strange spiders spun their gossamer webs and stared down with beady eyes. Kettles were aboil upon a makeshift crane. In a small recess, before a hand-made desk, sat alone an aged man, his flowing white beard reaching past the tabletop, obscuring the fastenings of the cloak that fell across his shoulders and was gathered upon his chest. His gaunt hands played with a queer metallic pen; and on a sheet of white paper before him there were a few lines of scrawling script. The uncertain light of the fire had been augmented, in the niche, by a candle, down whose sides the wax had run until the desktop and the nearest leg were smeared and streaked with it.

"Who should have thought that Man would live to see his proud race reduced to this state?" the old man had written. "Emerging from the primordial slime at the beginning, we took refuge in caves, and from them moved outward to work our destiny. Now, sinking down again into that eternal night from which there is no return, having again fled to Mother Earth's great caves—"

The end of the sentence trailed off into an illegible scrawl. As if there was much more to be written, but little enthusiasm for the writing of it, the author of the paragraph was toying with his pen; now putting the thick end of it to his lips contemplatively, now drumming with it upon the wooden top of the desk, now permitting it to lie idle in his fingers as he gazed, somewhat anxiously, toward the open mouth of the cave.

At length, throwing the pen down upon the desk in disgust, he arose with great effort, and, taking a short walking stick from its place against the rough wall, began to make his way with difficulty toward the entrance and the pool. As he rose to his full height, it was plain that in his youth and middle age he had been a majestic figure. Tall, well proportioned even in age, his sharply chiseled face bespoke intelligence and the habit of authority. His skin, like that of the woman, was black, contrasting with the luxuriant full white beard. His clothing, like hers, was loose and flowing; such garments, typical of hot countries, permitting the maximum of air circulation beneath, and great freedom of movement. He carried with him a learned and august dignity, which seemed to be token a broad benevolence of spirit; but at the same time there was singular sadness and hopelessness in those eyes, which had already looked too long upon the death throes of his race.

From the table to the opening was but a short distance, but the old man took a long time to get so far. It was plain that the infirmities of age were heavy upon him; the legs that had borne him faithfully through a long life would not carry him much longer. Beside the entrance there was a stool, so placed as to permit the occupant a broad view of the entire cavern. Reaching this he sank wearily upon it, keeping his staff in hand, and for half an hour he stared gloomily toward the other end of the lake.

"Now I am monarch of all the Earth," he mumbled to himself, ironically. "This is my kingdom!"

Time passed slowly. Still the woman did not return. Oppressed by the silence and the waiting, the old man again rose and made his way back into the cave, toward the fire, dragging the stool with him. He set it down before the blaze, and rested again, his feet and hands spread out to catch the warmth.

He looked around him in the cave, which the fire had lighted up. There was near at hand a stock of fuel, the dried stalks and roots of the cavern's chief vegetable growth. It burned eagerly, with much snapping and crackling, exuding an inflammable oil, which helped to sustain the blaze. Also, there was a stock of food, from the deep lake's yield of unnamed fish, and a quantity of the root of an edible plant. Unpleasant to eat and use, these things nevertheless would sustain man's life for a long time to come. It would be possible, perhaps, to rear whole families here, to build a new race.

The old man seemed lost in thought, revolving in his mind a weighty problem which had troubled him often before. At length he hobbled back to the littered desk with determination. He took the pen between his fingers, and dipping it into a horn of ink, began to write.

"If there shall ever be another living being," he wrote, "to read these lines, besides my son and daughter, who with me are the sole survivors of the Earth's millions, let them place the blame, if there be any, upon my head for what I am about to do. My days upon this wretched Earth are numbered. I foresee the end; and shall be content if only I am permitted to watch the sun go down once more in the free open air. But as to my son and daughter, alas, in them resides the destiny of this cursed remnant of the race.

"Living in a cave like beasts, we reach back after many generations to the moral values of the beast. For, though I have fought the idea with all the force in my being, trying to summon up all those reserves of moral fortitude, repugnance and horror which have existed in our people since the dawn of time, the monstrous thing I am about to command does not seem monstrous to me, now, but necessary. Necessary! The last struggle of a dying race, which even at the end cries out for life, is making me the instrument of its desire.

"My son and daughter are the only human beings upon this Earth capable of continuing the race.

"Continuing it whither? I know not. The end, it seems, must be inevitable. This generation or the next—it makes little difference in the end. Still, I cannot bear the thought of its perishing utterly so soon, while there is yet power in my command, and in their bodies, to carry it on.

"Perhaps, who knows, our messages beseeching aid from other planets may yet be answered—even after so long a time of waiting.

"God of the Universe, if indeed there be such a One—I ask forgiveness—"

All Hope Gone

THE pen dropped from his trembling hands and rolled to the stony floor. He did not reach for it, but stared straight before him at the hard wall. "Strength, strength," he muttered. "I must be firm!"

He heard hurried footsteps along the path outside. Someone was walking there, coming toward the cave.

With a quick motion he blotted the fresh ink on the paper before him, and covered what he had written with a clean white sheet. Then he composed himself with an effort, and turned half around to face the entrance, with a weary smile, partly mechanical, upon his lips.

He did not notice, when the girl appeared at the portal and turned to walk inside, that her hair was disheveled, her clothing soiled and torn, her torch gone. He did not see the horror in her eyes or the signs of weeping. He observed only that she was out of breath, as if she had run a great distance.

"You have been gone—a long time, Nina," he said kindly. "I was a little worried for a time. No doubt you found everything all right with Nino. When is he coming in?"

The girl hesitated a moment before answering, as if choosing her words.

"Father," she said at length, quietly, "Nino—is dead!"

"Dead?"

Despite his age and weakness, the old man rose up to his full height from the stool, and raised his trembling arms above his head in a gesture of the utmost grief and despair. His face was suddenly drawn and seamed; his eyes betrayed the shock the news had given him. He sank back upon his seat again. It was some minutes before he could speak.

The girl stood silently by the fire, looking into it stoically, as if life had taught her to take all thing's calmly.

"When I went out to look for him," she said after a time, "I hurried down the passageway toward Mansende and the old building where Nino used to take up his watch of the valley and the beacon tower, waiting for an answer to our radio signals to the other planets. The passageway, you remember, runs at an even level underground to a point below the building; then it goes upward by a long flight of stairs.

"I had no difficulty getting nearly to the end of the passage. But there, almost within sight of the lowermost flight of stairs, I was assailed by a frightful cloud of fine white dust. Fearing that something terrible had happened, I ran on through the choking stuff, guarding my breathing as well as I could, and began to make my way up the dark flights, now covered on the lower portions with debris. I saw that the shaft way no longer showed the spot of light which used to mark the upper opening.

"The piles of debris grew thicker as I climbed. I found one place where the stairs had given way. A little farther up, a great stone blocked my path. I laid my torch down and struggled with it, finally succeeding in moving it enough to let me through.

"Then I perceived what had happened. The old building, giving a way to age and the pressure of Earth, at last had fallen in. Crawling through cracks and dark holes, I finally reached the top of the stairs, and there I found—Nino! He was dead, crushed horribly beneath two huge blocks, which had formed part of the arch of the roof. Apparently he had heard the building begin to fall, and had sought to make the passage when it was too late."

She paused. The old man wrung his hands.

"My God," he moaned. "Why should it have been Nino? Why not my body, worthless as it is, instead of his?"

The girl, evidently misunderstanding, hurried to his side and stroked his hair and face, comforting him.

"We must not lose our courage now," she reminded him softly. "We two—alone—must face it out!"

"Yes, yes," he murmured. "Perhaps it was intended so—"

Then with a sudden motion he reached his hand out to the desk. His fingers closed upon the papers there, and with a convulsive grasp he crumpled them. The girl had not noticed, or she had pretended not to see, what he had written.

"Nino did not die without leaving a message," she said after a pause. "He had some paper with him and a pencil. While he lay dying upon the stone floor he wrote a note to us. This slip was in his hand when I found him."

She reached into her tunic and brought out a crumpled page. Upon it, scrawled by one evidently in haste and in intense pain, was this message:

"You can't get out this way or any other unless help comes from the outside. But do not give up. Today I saw a great white bird alight upon the beacon tower, move the thumb, and take the message, with which he flew away. I think—"

The remainder of the sentence was obliterated by a dark red stain. Holding it to the light they saw that it had never been completed.

"Was the passage blocked as he said?" asked the old man.

The girl nodded.

"I could not get farther than his body. There is no chance to force our way through that pile of stones," she replied.

"Then we are trapped. We can't get out."

"But perhaps—the white bird—"

The man shook his head.

"That's nonsense," he said. "Delirium."

"Nino was hardly the kind to lose his head, even if he was suffering."

"I know; but Nina, there are no birds on the Earth any longer. Our people shot many of them for food; the others died of thirst. Poor Nino—poor Nino!"

Doomed

THE old man's grief was seriously affecting him. He put his head upon the stained and greasy desk, burying it in his arms, while the waxen candle flared and flickered nearby, its melted substance running in long ridges down its side.

"But, whether it was a bird or not," the girl exclaimed, "something took the cylinder and sprang the trap."

Her father raised his head and stared at her blankly. "Nina," he asked, "is it true? The trap was sprung?"

She nodded. "When I left Nino I went down the other passage to the tower. The image had been sent down the shaft by its weight's drawing up the ladder, as we had arranged. The trapdoor at the top is closed, but it can he opened by anyone capable of reasoning out how to free the cylinder. Perhaps the stranger did not stop to read, or needed a translator."

"The message was taken!"

The old man for the moment forgot his sorrow in the new excitement. "You're sure the cylinder is gone? The jointed thumb had been moved?"

His daughter nodded. "I looked at it carefully," she said.

"Then it was an intelligent creature who found it! Was there any sign of livings about?"

"I climbed up the stairways and the ladder to the top, and opened the trapdoor so that I could examine the whole valley, and even the edges of the surrounding cliffs. But I could see nothing. There are not even tracks!"

"That's strange—"

"Unless our visitor was extremely light, or unless he only flew, and never alighted. Nino wrote of a white bird."

The old man smoothed out his manuscript thoughtfully and returned it to the desk.

"In any case," he said, "we have not yet been rescued, though hours must have passed since they found it."

He then took his daughter's hand. "Now there are only two of us," he murmured, "and soon there will be—only you, Nina."

She shrank in horror from the gloom and silence of the cavern, but she did not reply. Instead, she put her strong young arm about his shoulders, and held his head close to her.

"Oh, help will come," she declared after a time. "I'm sure of it."

Aiding him tenderly, she guided the old mall across the uneven floor to his stool before the fire. Then, throwing upon the blaze a fresh bundle of fuel, she nestled down beside him to watch the flames leap high, to take solace with him in the friendly warmth, which had cheered the members of the human race from the dawn of mankind.

In the dark crannies of the cave, strange insects watched these doomed members of a once proud race, their figures silhouetted against the yellow miracle that they had brought with them into the cavern.

Outside, in the valley, a little wind had sprung up; and the sweeping dust came cascading over the high walls of the hollow, to continue covering up the tomb of Man and to erase from the Earth the last marks he had made upon it.

CHAPTER FOUR
Dolmician, the Emperor

THERE was a long procession winding through the silvery streets of Nealoma, accompanied by the deep booming sound of *Anathryptic* drums, the sweet, sharp tones of the *nantigore* played with a muted bell, and the ripple of many feet moving rhythmically on the hard surfaces; and there was, too, the rustle of broad wings. Bravely uniformed guards, beribboned like pages in an Ardathian court, passed and repassed overhead. On either side of the line of march—their wings folded but ready, and in their hands the short *zythus* which had done such mighty work in the campaigns against the Helvae—stood the proud legionaries of Pleida, keeping back the crowds who pressed too close in seeking a glimpse of the daring travelers.

The air was close and singularly hot, despite the distance of the sun; the ground was warm. Heat seemed to come outward from the core of this world, turning the moisture of the soil to vapor as it came, and filling the atmosphere with quivering waves. Great as was their distance from the sun, the streets were filled with a brilliant light, of peculiar blue-green intensity, greatly unlike that which played upon the face of Tellus. It was the quality and nature of the Pleidan atmosphere that changed the sunlight, straining out many of the red rays, and emphasizing the blues and greens. In addition, there penetrated to the surface much more of the actinic rays than reached the surface of the dead planet; and the bleaching effect of these rays was everywhere apparent.

It was not noticed, however, by the race of short, squat phlegmatic people who inhabited the major portion of the planet. Even the great weight of every common thing, more than two and half times as great as it would have been on

Tellus, did not seem to trouble these beings. With the aid of gravity nullifiers, they flitted to and fro, either in the air or on the ground, with little apparent effort, where a Tellurian man would have been made helpless by his own weight.

The procession moved through a carnival of little multi-colored balloons and bright paper discs between the ranks of cheering gaily-clad citizens who lined the route on either side. The chief streets of the city shone with pageantry. Crowds upon the high rooftops shouted welcoming cries through megaphones. Bands played and accented the rhythms of the march. But an observer might have perceived that such emotion as the people showed was simulated; that, between their exclamations, their faces relaxed into that stony gloomy mold for which Pleidans are noted.

Ahead marched the *Bala*, lifting their arms rhythmically above their heads, and indicating that an event of importance to the whole universe were about to occur. The special guards came next, marching three deep before and after the jeweled guests of honor, who moved in double file, looking neither to the left nor right; for it was improper to acknowledge the plaudits of the crowd until respect had been paid to the Emperor.

Straight ahead, before the marching lines, stretched the great avenue; and at its end, upreared against the green-gold sky, stood the broad, blocky palace of Dolmician. The terraced steps ran upward to portals guarded on either side by tawny *zelinx* in precious metal, the symbol at once of authority and cruelty. Beyond the portal opened the hallway, nearly as wide as the street, and at the far end of it was the auditorium where sat the mighty Dolmician himself. Enrobed with garments signifying his power and degree, he awaited in the Emperor's box, the marchers. His receiving ring gleamed upon his fat third finger, the jewel out: and a smile of welcome was enforced upon his countenance. His short, squat figure seemed more a block of carved stone than a living man.

At the terraced steps the guards marched ahead; the line parted into two columns between which passed the honored men. Salvarius Carde was first to enter the presence of the Emperor. In his hand he carried the metal Tellurian cylinder, now beribboned and much polished in an attempt to make its appearance more acceptable. After him came the others of the expedition, with Allus Marce, the youngest, bringing up the rear. On the bodies of all were the dull metallic boxes holding the gravity-nullifying equipment. They knelt in deference.

"Arise, Men of Pleida!" boomed Dolmician: "You who have trodden stardust need kneel no more before an Emperor!"

At that the courtiers and nobles, of whom there were myriads lining the audience chamber, set up a great roaring noise. Heavy throbbing music from unseen sources poured out into the great hall and, as though the blessing of the Emperor had indeed been translated into sight and scent, there came dropping from the arched and darkened vault overhead, the brilliant, tinted petals of the night-blooming *antinone*, accompanied by clouds of perfume.

Salvarius Carde, all smiles at this triumph, stepped forward, the cylinder from Tellus in his hand.

"Behold the last message of the Tellurians," he declared. "We have preserved it for your Serene Majesty that it may be translated at your command. As for the Tellurian race of which tradition speaks—it has disappeared."

"What? Disappeared?"

"There were no traces of anything alive; though we searched diligently over the whole planet, and especially in the deep, dried-up basin where this cylinder was found."

"Ah," replied the Emperor, apparently but little disappointed. "Trust Salvarius Carde to do everything that was necessary. Had these Earthmen had such a leader among them, they never would have perished; he would have found a way."

Carde's Story

SALVARIUS bowed low at this declaration of his ruler's esteem. "Perhaps so, Sire," he replied. "But I really feel, O mighty Dolmician, that you praise me more than I deserve."

"Not at all. On the contrary, we feel that your obvious talents will stand us in very good stead in certain enterprises we are even now contemplating."

"I thank you, Sire. But, experienced though I am, neither I nor any member of my family, so far as I know, has ever succeeded in creating water where the elements necessary to its existence were absent."

"Water?"

"Yes, Sire. It was from lack of it that the Tellurians perished from their Earth."

It was apparent that the Emperor was no longer interested in the Tellurians.

"Well, well," he declared, pursing his lips sorrowfully. "What a pity!"

"But may I tell your Serene Majesty of the circumstances connected with the finding of this cylinder, which I believe contains a history of that unfortunate race?" persisted Salvarius Carde.

"Yes, yes—of course."

Allus Marce flushed with excitement, remembering that it was he and none other who had discovered the relic. Now would the Emperor learn that there were other good men besides Salvarius Carde!

It was difficult for him to keep his place. With the eagerness and inexperience of youth, he wanted to move forward and stand beside Salvarius Carde during the recital of the tale, perhaps to tell it himself—as was his right. None but he had seen the valley that had been once the bottom of the sea. He alone had mounted the crystal tower, wrested the message from the graven figure, and watched it descend, plummet-like, mocking him with its inscrutable smile.

He aroused himself from these reflections to perceive that Salvarius Carde had already launched upon the story. Suddenly Allus Marce's ears burned; his face grew red with anger and indignation. For, as he listened, it was apparent that Salvarius Carde, without even mentioning the true discoverer's name, was telling the tale as though he himself had found the lost valley and the treasure it contained.

"Adjusting my portable gravity-nullifier on my back—for as your Majesty knows, the force of gravity on Tellus is considerably less than on Pleida, I flew across the planet. I came at length," Salvarius Carde continued, "to a valley deeper than any other in the pitted surface of Tellus. There, in its bottom, partly covered by sand, are the ruins of a great stone city. And upreared in the center of the city, its base already covered over with the sand so that a door no longer shows, is a giant obelisk. Upon the top of the obelisk was a carved figure, purporting to be that of a Tellurian man. In the figure's stony hand was this cylinder, plainly intended as a message to anyone visiting Tellus and wishing to learn the history of the race that had perished there.

"As you may be certain, Sire, I approached the figure firmly and wrenched the cylinder from its grasp. I would have brought the figure also with me to Pleida, in order that it might be mounted in one of our mighty museums here; but an unfortunate accident prevented that. The mortar that cemented it to the obelisk's top was aged and crumbling. I should guess that it had stood there, exposed to the fury of the elements, for hundreds of years. As I took the cylinder, the mortar at last gave way and, before I could catch it, the statue had tumbled over the side and dashed itself to pieces against the ground.

"Your Majesty will understand that I regretted this loss exceedingly; so much so, in fact, that I sat down beside the pieces on the hard ground and gave myself up to grief for half an hour. At the end of that time, perceiving that the loss was irretrievable, I left the fragments where they had fallen and hastened to the spaceship. There the other members of the expedition, having spent many fruitless days in searching for relics, gathered around me. We wrenched the cylinder open and learned that there were indeed writings inside; though of such strange characters that we could not understand anything of their nature."

Allus Marce gasped in astonishment at the effrontery of this narrative; and would have burst out in denial, had not one of the other members of the expedition, perceiving the young man's perturbation, placed a hand on his shoulder and whispered softly into his ear.

"You must not—now!" the other remarked. "To disturb the equanimity of the Emperor at this time would cast no discredit on Salvarius Carde's story, and would only do your own reputation and future irreparable harm. There are others who know the truth besides yourself. Wait until the proper time comes before you declare yourself."

Allus Marce breathed fast, but kept his peace. He nodded to his companion, who smiled momentarily. Then both of them turned their eyes steadfastly toward the Emperor, who was regarding the ribboned cylinder, poising it in his pudgy hands.

"Call in the official translators!" he ordered imperiously.

There was a hubbub among the servants of the court. In a moment the seven translators were brought, each dressed in a robe that signified the degrees he held and the exploits that had endeared him to the Emperor.

"Inside this metal container," said Dolmician when they were all assembled, "I am reliably informed that there are sheets bearing a message from the extinct races of the planet Tellus. I want that message translated as soon as possible, and the report of its contents made directly to me."

Honors Bestowed

THE eldest of the translators, finding the cap already loosened by the efforts of Salvarius Carde's mechanics, unscrewed it with his hand and brought the message out. The six others gathered quickly and somewhat anxiously around him, scrutinizing the sheets. Then they held a short conference, and at length the eldest spoke.

"All-powerful Emperor," he began in his humblest manner, "we here see that a task of no mean proportions has been set for us. For we have neither key nor experience with this language or these characters. It will take time to translate such a message as this."

"How much time?" inquired the Emperor impatiently.

"No man could with certainty tell you that. It may take years; it may take lifetimes."

The Emperor frowned.

"Too long! Too long!" he thundered. "I will have no such delay. A day or two at most should do the work. See, there are fewer than two dozen sheets. Lifetimes, indeed!"

He waved the uncomfortable translators toward the gallery door. "Don't waste my time," he bellowed after them. "Bring me a translation before two days are gone, or I'll put the work in better hands!"

Smiling, he then turned toward Salvarius Carde, who was standing expectantly at the head of the band of explorers. The Emperor clapped his jeweled hands.

"Salvarius Carde," he exclaimed in the high, singsong voice appointed for ceremonials. "I do now appoint you a noble among nobles, with the title 'Guardian of the Universe'." He clapped his hands. "The robes!"

Four squat blocks of humanity, called pages, bearing the garments of power and the symbols of the new estate, appeared from the sides of the great hall and bestowed upon the pleased and preening Salvarius the symbols of his rank, while the auditorium rang with the monotonous, lifeless applause.

"And as for the other members of your expedition," continued the Emperor, ponderously, "them do I entitle Honorable; recognizing that, though they brought no relics of the people of Tellus, they nevertheless have been of some assistance to you in the work which you have accomplished so well. As a reward for accompanying you, I will cause their names to be inscribed on a table of imperishable metal, and the tablet to be placed in plain view in the main hall of my palace; so that future generations may come and look upon it."

"How generous is the Emperor!" cried the hundreds of nobles present, perceiving that there was universal disappointment in the faces of the followers of Salvarius Carde. So loudly did they cry it that the Emperor himself smiled in their direction, acknowledging their praise. With that the music struck up again, and the great Dolmician arose and turned the jewel of his ring inward toward the palm; signifying thus that the ceremony was over.

The nobles were hurrying from their places to greet the proud and beaming Salvarius Carde, who now held a station equal to and, in some respects, greater than their own; and the little band of Salvarius Carde's followers was dispersing in silence, when a commotion in the gallery brought them all to a halt.

A page hurried in, and knelt at the feet of the retiring Emperor, giving him a message. Dolmician read it; and turning to the throng in the hall, he raised his hand for quiet.

"The translators have already rendered the Tellurian message into our own tongue," he declared. "Return to your places and they will read it to us."

The murmuring and congratulations ceased. A sea of expectant faces turned upward toward the gallery in strained attention. The eldest of the translators appeared, followed by the others. With heavy gravity they moved to the dais before the Emperor and bowed.

"You have made a fair and accurate translation?" inquired the ruler.

"We have, Sire."

"You have not taken advantage of the fact that no one else here can read the message, and thus give the lie to you?"

For a moment the spokesman faltered, but his reply was steady enough:

"We have not, O Illustrious Emperor."

"Then read the message from the Tellurians!"

The eldest of the translators unrolled a large scroll upon which had been written a hasty text.

"Before I begin, Sire," he said, "I want to explain that ours is a very compact language, compared with that of the Tellurians. Consequently, what they took pages to write, we have here been able to render into two or three paragraphs. They are as follows:

" 'Mourn not for us, O other peoples of the Universe; for we of the planet Tellus have chosen to die by our own hands in shame because our bodies and our minds are neither so beautiful nor so powerful as the bodies and minds of the planet Pleida.

"'For many generations we were a happy people, but now we are wretched with jealousy. A band of our explorers, cruising the ether, landed upon Pleida, and brought back such reports of the beauty of that world, the strength and intelligence of her people, the justice and might of her Emperor, the strictness of her laws and the mercy with which they are administered, that we are consumed with envy and despair; and we have chosen to die and leave this planet for habitation by those mighty beings, more worthy than we.

" 'So, if any men from Pleida find this message, and bear it away, and translate it, take it with our greetings and felicitations to the great Emperor Dolmician, and tell him that this little world is his to do with as he pleases, for we are relinquishing it to him!' "

When he had finished, the translator rolled up his scroll again, fastened it dexterously with a bright ribbon, and handed it to the Emperor. The nobles applauded thunderously. Dolmician beamed.

"Well, now," said he. "That is a noble message. These Tellurians must have been a fine people, after all!"

Allus Marce, with the rashness of youth, raised his arm for permission to speak. It was granted him.

"But what do the Tellurians say with regard to the absence of all water from their Earth?" he inquired.

The translators appeared confused, and avoided his eyes and those of Salvarius Carde and the other voyagers.

"As a matter of fact," said their spokesman at length. "The message does not mention the subject, as you have observed. The Tellurians, in paying this compliment to our mighty Emperor, did not bring up the matter of water at all."

"And quite rightly," chimed in the Emperor, turning his ring back again toward his palm, and dismissing the audience.

"I will have this translation framed for the public hall; and the metal cylinder and the original sheets shall be placed in the Royal Museum."

Allus Marce, with the others, passed out into the street. He said nothing, but his body was trembling with anger and indignation.

CHAPTER FIVE
The House of Allus

AROUND the ancient sun wheeled the planet Jupiter (known to its inhabitants as Pleida) making his journey once in eleven years ten and a third months, as time was once measured on Tellus. His great volume, more than thirteen hundred times that of the tiny, dead planet, marked him lord of the solar retinue. His cold journey through space was performed eternally at a distance of nearly five hundred million miles from the source of his light. Yet his face was not chilled, for from his heart came the great warmth of inner fires, which served eternally to keep his inhabitants at livable temperatures. This was similarly true for his larger satellites.

These companions were nine in number, four of which were inhabited. The largest, called by its inhabitants Neina, had a diameter of 3,550 Tellurian miles, exceeding the planet Mercury and approaching Mars in size. Another, called Quena, measured 2,100 miles in diameter; and thus was somewhat larger than the single moon of Tellus.

Upon the satellites existed the highest and oldest civilization of this strange system of moons and mother planet. Upon Neina had developed that unique race of winged beings which later inhabited the four greater satellites, and finally, even Pleida itself. But now was Pleida the ruler, and the satellites were subject territory in government as well as in physical relationship. On the larger body, the race not only had grown rapidly and prospered but, yielding to the subtle influences exerted by the tremendous gravitation, the hot, damp climate, and the great distances, had changed to a brutal and selfish character, interested only in ruling and in military prowess.

From this branch of the race had sprung Salvarius Carde and like other native Pleidans he was short and sturdy, heavy-boned and phlegmatic. But Allus Marce, slender and refined and of a certain delicacy, as befitted a native of the small, light satellites, had come from Neina. It might be said that, although Pleidans had little difficulty in navigating the surface of the moons, the inhabitants of the moons were obliged to have the intense gravitational pull thoroughly nullified by portable apparatus before they could travel over Pleida.

Not long after the scene at Dolmician's court, on a day when anger was still seething within him, Allus Marce stood upon the polished floor of the audience room in the house of his father. Before him, on a raised dais, the aged patriarch of the House of Allus sat enthroned in a chair of bright metal, with the robes of his degree and the seal of his authority upon him; for the family of which he was the head had vast estates, and ranked among the greatest nobility of the four moons.

The old man raised a kindly, withered hand.

"You have now wandered farther afield than any of the illustrious line of Allus before you," he began. "You have surveyed the stars in their courses; you have trodden planets where never a native son of the Pleidan system had planted his foot before. You have breathed the air even of far-off Tellus; you have flown over her wasted surfaces. Such adventuring should cure the most insatiable wanderlust."

The young man nodded.

"And yet—" he said. "Not satisfied, after so much?" The patriarch raised his eyebrows questioningly. "Don't you think it's time that you prepare to take up my work here, since I shall soon be compelled to relinquish it? Is it not time that, as heir to the headship of Allus and its properties, you took a sterner view of life?"

Marce cast his eyes down, unwilling by word or gesture to
anger his father or to betray how little he regarded the sacred
and age-old functions of a family head. Compared with the
more glorious existence of discovery and exploration, it
seemed flat and tasteless, as though a strong man should vol-
untarily undergo the amputation of his wings, so that always
thereafter he must walk instead of fly, creep on the ground
rather than beat out the *elons* magnificently in the sky.

"But I am still young—" he objected.

The patriarch regarded him critically through half-closed
eyes, turning over in his mind many quiet reflections.

"Youth." He said at length," is no excuse, except perhaps
for inexperience. You are you young—yes! But it is time,
nevertheless, that you took to yourself a wife and settled
down to the care and understanding of your life's duties,
bringing forth heirs to the House of Allus."

"I don't want a wife," Marce replied, his face flushed with
emotion. "In all Pleida I have not seen a woman I wish to
marry!"

His father smiled indulgently.

"Where else then?" he inquired. "In all your travels to
other worlds—have you seen anyone whom you'd marry
rather than the women of your own race?"

Marce shook his head. "But I have heard of one," he said
bluntly. "I have heard of one whom I would marry, if she
would have me—and if she still lives."

"What?"

"The fact is," said Marce, turning the subject, "I am not
yet ready to settle down. I know what you think—that I'm
no good, that I haven't the courage to manage your estates,
that I'm a weakling and worthless as an heir. Actually, it is
because other considerations trouble me that I cannot give up
my freedom now. Father, I tell you this: my visit to Tellus
has fired me with determination to visit it again. There is a

mystery in Tellus that has not been solved. I cannot reconcile the disappearance of all its water and its race of men as well with the legend preserved in our family that, not so very long ago, Tellurians visited us, staying beneath this very roof as our guests. Why did the Earth race die out so quickly? What has happened there?"

"Why didn't you satisfy yourself while you were there?"

"With Salvarius Carde in command?" Marce's voice trembled with his pent-up anger.

"Why not? He is a soldier and a gentleman."

"And a thief and poltroon as well, who covers himself with glory at other men's expense!"

Marce Tells All

THE patriarch suddenly became dignified and cold, as though the attitude of his son toward one so greatly honored by the Emperor had appeared also a personal affront to himself.

"You will remember," he said, "that Salvarius Carde is now a ranking noble, and as such deserving of your respect; however much you may in private doubt the wisdom of the Emperor in so honoring him. Further, it would be well for you to keep in mind that only after repeated urging on my part, Salvarius Carde, who is my friend, took you with him on the trip. He felt that you would be too young, that you would be a hindrance and a source of danger. You should show gratitude, at least!"

Allus Marce listened patiently, but his eyes were blazing.

"My father," he replied, "for all these things which you have done for me, and for all the things Salvarius Carde has done for me, I am indeed greatly indebted. But has Salvarius Carde reported to you, since our return, whether I was a help or a hindrance on the expedition?"

"No, he has not."

"Neither did he mention me, or anyone else in the expedition, to the Emperor; but rather sought to take all the credit and all the glory of the whole trip upon himself."

"Well?"

"The fact is, my father, that it was I and not Salvarius Carde who discovered the message cylinder. The leader of our expedition, who took so much credit upon himself, was never near the place; and neither was any other member of the party. The 'facts' as reported by Salvarius Carde to the Emperor were false and distorted; and all the other members of the expedition know it. They are now afraid to tell the truth, only for fear that Salvarius, the nobleman, and your friend would harm them for it. I tell you, father, just as these Pleidans here borrowed our music and our art and made such dull, flat things of them" (no Pleidan is naturally musical) "so they wish to steal the glory due us."

The head of the House of Allus stared speechlessly at his son. Then, rising from his chair, he stood like a tower of white flame upon the dais, resentment and wrath in his every gesture.

"Marce, is this thing you have told me the truth?"

The young man nodded silently.

"And can you bring me proof of it? Will the others of the expedition, if secretly questioned here, bear you out?"

"The members of our own race will. The Pleidans—I can't answer for them."

For many generations the people of the satellites had been ground down by the despotic Pleidan rulers who had gained control over them. They now groaned beneath their burdens—the cruelties, the inequalities, and the frequent plundering expeditions of the nobles of Pleida. The Pleidans had fallen into a contemptuous attitude toward the satellites and their peoples. Neina they called by the undignified name

Noninus, a diminutive with a somewhat deprecatory meaning. The other satellites received similar slurs: and were forced, as well, to pay tribute to the Emperor and to be forever at the mercy of his capricious will.

As the result the inhabitants of Neina and those of the other moons had developed among themselves a fierce, secret pride. The inhabitants of Helva, the fourth moon, had in fact repeatedly rebelled against the authority of the Emperor; and such fierce fighters were they that despite the power and wealth of the Pleidan armies, they had actually set up self-government of a kind, though it cost them heavily in men and wealth to maintain it.

THE relations between the House of Allus and the Emperor had always been tenuous and a trifle hostile, particularly since the time of Marce's grandfather, when the ruling Emperor of the time had seen fit arbitrarily to deprive him of some of his lands. That his father, driven at last to extreme resentment, might someday be induced to break with the central power and lead the peoples of the satellites in a concerted revolution, had long been a hope of Marce. In many ways he felt the superiority of his family to the decadent rulers of the planet. Though traffic and intercourse between the moons and Pleida was comparatively easy, with the improved space cars of the system, and travel frequent, the widely divergent nature of life on each body tended rapidly to develop divergent characteristics. From generation to generation, the principal stocks of the four moons and those of the planet had grown farther apart, in appearance, tastes, habits of thought and modes of living.

Pleida, with her gravitational pull about fifteen times that of the satellites, had invested every object on her surface with frightful weight; this consideration alone was enough to condition all plant and animal life. It gave even to architecture and abstract design a decided tendency toward massiveness and broadness, which was highly distasteful to the inhabitants of the moons. Similarly, the men of the mother planet grew stouter and shorter; their bones heavy and thick; their flesh ran to grossness and their minds to cruelty and lasciviousness. Upon the lighter satellites, the prevailing lines were slender, extending upward. The buildings were tall, well proportioned. The plants were waving fronds, the people slender and white, given to personal graces and the practice of refined arts. That these varieties had actually developed from the same original race in a few thousand generations might seem to the chance observer impossible. Yet, as the extreme adaptability of the Pleidan race had made it possible for the same people to live on worlds of such divergent characteristics, so had it also permitted these more permanent changes to take place rapidly.

Some of these considerations were going through Allus Marce's mind as he stood there before his father. The patriarch, conquering his feelings for the time being, at length descended. Laying a hand on Marce's shoulder he said, in a voice that trembled, "My son, perhaps I have wronged you. If you have been thus insulted, then the House of Allus has been insulted, and we must repay!"

"Yes," Marce replied, "but we must do it shrewdly. We must be sure that we shall succeed—for it is not so much the insult to me or to our house that counts. It is the happiness of our people!"

A Rescue from Jupiter
by Gawain Edwards

(Illustration by Paul)

"We learn that out of the cold blackness of space they came to us in a space ship of crude design, but supplied with what seemed to be unlimited power. To go to Pleida they dared not."

CHAPTER SIX
The Visit of the Tellurians

THE old man was leading the way. Allus Marce followed him silently. They came at length to a locked, metallic door. Fumbling in his pouch, the elder Allus drew out a paper; reading a notation in cipher, he turned some dials on the lock. The door moved back on croaking hinges and revealed a small, dimly lighted room in which were several chests, dust-covered from remaining undisturbed through many years.

"Here are the records of your fathers before me," the old man began. "In these chests lies the history of our House; and an illustrious history it has been."

For a moment the patriarch was silent, as if watching the effect of this pronouncement upon his son. Marce, if he was stirred, made no sign. His father, after a time, went on.

"I have brought you here," he said, "to tell you what you should know about the visit of the Tellurians to Neina, many, many *deismas* ago."

Marce's eyes sparkled. He waited for his father to continue.

"From these records, so carefully preserved and handed down in secret in our family, we learn that out of the cold blackness of space they came to us, in a spaceship crude of design, but supplied with what seemed unlimited power. To go on to Pleida they dared not, because their great weight would have pinned them helplessly to the ground, unable to move a hand or finger to set their machine in motion to return them to Tellus. So they stopped with us. Here, while conditions were greatly different from their own Earth's, they were able to live. Their weight here was only about one-sixth that on their own world.

"Our house was then, as now, the greatest on Neina. Our forefather received these visitors with royal pomp; for despite their strangeness of features and mind, their inadaptability, and their state of winglessness, he was greatly pleased with them. After a time he learned to converse with them in a mixed speech, partly theirs and partly ours. They, in turn, seemed greatly pleased with life on Neina. One member in particular, who seemed to be the leader, became virtually one of us. There was only one thing that seemed to trouble these men on our satellite. When they came to us their skins were of a tan color; but the rays of light we receive, which as you know tend to bleach everything except the plants, soon turned them almost as white as ourselves.

"The head of the House of Allus, who was then a young man, seemed pleased by this change; since he felt that it greatly improved the appearance of his visitors, however much it destroyed their uniqueness. They, however, felt otherwise, and they expressed the hope frequently that their strange color would return to them when they departed again for home. They explained that all the men of Tellus were of a dark color, and that they would be ridiculed if they were white; which seems to me preposterous and perhaps a tale they had invented to keep us from learning the real truth.

"At any rate, they stayed with us a long time—so long, in fact, that one of the ladies of the court, herself of noble birth, fell in love with their leader. She was greatly given to his company. This feeling he evidently returned, for at length he expressed a desire to marry her. When both agreed, our forefather called physicians, had them examined as, of course, is customary before marriage. The physicians reported this curious thing: that, though they had come from totally different stocks, developing not only in different environments but even on different planets, there was no biological law against their marriage; and it was even believed possible that they might bear fine, healthy children. The ceremony took place; though the other members of the expedition from Tellus were much opposed to it and tried by various means to dissuade their leader.

"Nevertheless, the marriage was consummated. As might have been expected, the union of a member of the Neinan nobility with a member of another race was widely discussed and protested. Many ignorant persons, especially of Pleida, letting prejudices outweigh their better judgment, hypocritically appeared to consider it a kind of bestiality and heartily condemned not only the principals to the marriage, but the reigning member of Allus as well. Finally the word spread even to the court on Pleida; and the Emperor, a man fully as irascible and no less impulsive than the present ruler, took occasion to censure our progenitor severely.

"Feeling both on Pleida and Neina became heated. The Tellurians, sensing the impending disorder, begged their leader either to forsake his bride and return with them to their Earth or, if he insisted, to take her with him. She, however, was unwilling to leave her native world and he, faithful to his vows, refused to leave her.

"At length, upon a frightful night, the Tellurians mutinied, and applying power to their spaceship, went roaring off into space without their leader. A howling mob, perceiving that the Tellurians had gone, beat down the palace guards and entered this building, intent upon killing the woman who had (as they felt) defiled herself with this interplanetary love. They found, to their surprise, that the leader of the expedition from Tellus had not abandoned his bride, but that he was at their chamber door ready and willing to defend her from the mob.

"To make it brief, they fell upon him with all their weapons. Unarmed, he tore down the hangings of the chamber and beat them off with the metal rods. He flung at them the light furniture of the suite and, with the prodigious strength and cunning he had brought with him from his bigger world, he throttled many of his assailants with his bare hands. The rabble behind, unable to see what was holding them back, imagined for a time that the royal army had been called out to oppose their progress.

"When the guards did finally arrive, this terrific Tellurian, exhausted by his efforts and surrounded by the corpses of nearly a hundred members of our race whom he had slain to protect his bride, was dying of his wounds. It was then that the rabble realized what it had done. They saw that this Earthman was no beast, but a hero beside whom they were themselves but veriest weaklings and cowards. So, instead of further opposition to the guards, they decided to pick the dying man up upon their shoulders and honored him. And the woman he had married was honored thereafter as the purest of the satellite, and was held sacrosanct after he had died.

"Later she bore twin children, the offspring of the Tellurian man. *From one of them, Marce, from one of them we all descended.*"

"How long ago was this, father?"

"Almost five hundred deismas,* Marce."

"Then how is it that the knowledge of it is not accepted generally?"

"Since there were many wars during that time, the records of those day have been all but lost."

The old man paused, to see what effect his announcements had upon his son. Marce made no sign; but for a little while the elder was unable to continue.

"The other one was killed," said Marce quietly.

"Yes—but the story has been kept a secret for many generations. How did you know?"

---

* Eight hundred Earth years.

Marce Speaks

MARCE smiled enigmatically, but did not reply. His father went on: "So far as I can see, our only heritage from Tellus is great strength, endurance, and the curious way we have of thinking, which seems to Pleidans strange und sometimes unbalanced. We have a mightily intellectual curiosity, which is not particularly an attribute of our system's races. In fact, it seems to me that, through so many deismas, there have persisted traits given us by the Tellurians."

The two men, father and son, were for a long time silent after the elder had finished. If the patriarch had expected a more violent reaction, he gave no sign. At last, he spoke once more:

"It was the aftermath of this affair, when long after a man descended from a Tellurian came to the head of the House of Allus, that caused the Emperor in his wisdom and power to reduce the rank of our House. While we are still powerful, we are no longer, as we once were, rulers of Neina. It is one of the insults—there have been many since—to which we must reply, when the time comes."

Marce put his hand gently upon his father's sleeve.

"As a matter of fact," he said, "you expected me to be greatly moved when you told me that in my veins there flowed Tellurian blood. But I have long known the story you have just related to me here. Some time ago, I found the combination to this lock, and made my way into this very room. Here I found, among the old records of our forefather's day, not only the whole history of my descent but also, what is more important, a key made by him whereby the language of the Tellurians may be rendered into our own tongue with ease and exactness."

"What?" It was the elder who was startled at the revelation.

"It is true. Even before I left this house for Tellus I had learned this key as though it were my own language, so that if I were to meet any members of my race there I should be able, after a fashion, to converse with them. Unfortunately, there were none still alive, or so it seemed. There were only the scraps of paper in the metal cylinder."

The patriarch took his son affectionately by the shoulders, shaking him.

"And could you read the contents of the cylinder?"

Marce nodded.

"And yet you did not, because you did not care to let Salvarius Carde shine in greater glory than he had already taken upon himself?"

The younger man hesitated.

"Well—yes and no," he replied evasively. "That is—I could have read the manuscript—and I did!"

"You did read it? For whom?"

"For myself—and I alone know the translation."

"But the royal translators—"

The heir of Allus made a scornful gesture. "The liars!" he declared. "They forged a translation they knew would please the Emperor. What do they care for the truth?"

"But you—!"

"During the long journey from Tellus to Pleida, I had a premonition of the behavior of this Salvarius Carde, who was your friend. So, though he kept it closely guarded, I found occasion to borrow the cylinder and to make a copy of the contents secretly. These I have since translated fully. I have the translation here."

The older man clapped his hands together appreciatively.

"My boy!" he exclaimed. "And I thought you unfitted to inherit Allus!"

But Marce was not swept away by the enthusiasm that had seized his father. He replied seriously, looking directly and steadfastly into the old man's eyes.

"In fact, I am *not* fit to inherit Allus," he said. "At least not yet. For what I read in that paper, that tragic message of despair, from members of a race which may even now count me and my cousins as its only living members, has filled me with a wild desire to return to Tellus. That desire will—it must be fulfilled before the claims of Allus can affect me!"

"How so? How so?"

"I best can answer that by showing you the translation. But before I do so, my father, I must ask your secrecy until a fitting time has come to have the matter generally known."

"My boy, I promise!"

Marce reached into his tunic, and drew from a secret pocket a sheaf of closely written sheets.

"Here is the message, then," he said, "translated as it came from the cylinder."

His father took the papers; then paused for a moment, a suspicion entering his mind.

"Can you prove that the translation is genuine?"

The youth's eyes blazed.

"This from my father!" he exclaimed.

For a moment they regarded each other intensely. Something passed between them, a psychic wave, a union that grew from sympathy of the mind. At last the patriarch gripped the younger man's hand.

"I apologize from the bottom of my heart," he said. "It is the nature of the Pleidan race to be suspicious, even of one's relatives. Therefore, it is not among us a matter to become angry about, but to be accepted. Apparently, however, we inherit from the Tellurians a sense of personal honor not common in this larger world!"

Marce smiled in reply. "I hope so," he said.

CHAPTER SEVEN
The Message from Tellus

THE head of the House of Allus spread before him on a broad table the sheets containing the translation of the Tellurian message. Marce stood near him as he read:

"It may be that someone, in the endless space which stretches to infinity, some creature with a mind to understand and with compassion to feel for us in our last extremity, will find this message where it will be placed. It is too much to hope that when our plight is known there will still be some of us alive; but from the dawn of life men have always struggled upward, aided by undying hope, and hope is with us still.

"Therefore be it known that when this is written, toward the close of the year 8921 after the birth of Christ, from which the human race has been accustomed to date its time, there remain but a pitiful few of the mighty peoples which once ruled the Earth, and even sped among the planets. Feeling that the end is drawing near and is inevitable, we have completed the last monument that it now seems will ever be built to our race. Upon its top we have placed a figure not unlike one of us, and in that figure's hand will be put a cylinder containing this history and appeal. The grip upon the cylinder will be so maintained that it cannot be accidentally unfastened, or worked loose, except by a reasoning, intelligent being.

"It is impossible for anyone to understand our plight without some knowledge of our history. Ours is a race that has perished through its own sins. Prosperity was never good for us. We wantonly destroyed the gifts of nature. Once, when our globe was covered with trees, we cut them down. Our coal we used without regard to the consequences. Our oil we pumped out of the ground and burned away in pleasure, madness, and war.

"We were high livers. While we had the resources we maintained what we were accustomed to call a 'high standard of living.' For centuries preceding the year 7100, class distinctions had almost disappeared from among us. Mechanical appliances did most of the hard and necessary work. Through a series of socialistic coups early in the Twenty-Second Century, arrangements were made whereby all industries were administered by governmental groups for the benefit of the whole people. Thereafter, for hundreds of generations, peace and plenty seemed assured permanently. I will not say that there were no minor disasters. An earthquake in 4360 swallowed up Lower California and inundated the rich Imperial Valley. A revolution over the distribution of free power from the Texas oil fields generating plants* arose in the New England States of the North American Continent in 4889. There were disastrous fires, temporary power failures, and governmental scandals from time to time to stir up friction and cause bloodshed. But on the whole the peoples of the world, freed from the fundamental danger of hunger and want, lived in a veritable golden age. They appeared scarcely to realize that the good times would ultimately come to an end, after the natural resources upon which they were drawing so lavishly were used up.

"It took the Great War of 7560-7596 to make the spectre of want again a reality. Within the period of that cruel and bloody conflict our civilization was almost wiped out. Fuel and energy, which would have maintained the people in peace for generations, were shot away. Our wells were pumped dry. Coal seams that had previously been thought worthless were worked until they were exhausted. The last of the forests

---

*Which supplanted the coal-consuming power plants between 3500 and 3800.

went under the axe. When the war was over we saw that our former material prosperity, which had led us to these excesses after centuries of pleasant, existence on the Earth, could never be regained. The natural resources of the world, as we then understood them, were gone.

"Our fine systems of economics had likewise melted away. Collapsing one by one throughout the world, the benevolent cooperative agencies ceased their free distribution of comforts and necessities. Strong private entrepreneurs bought out the factories. Girls and children and men went to work in them, taking the places of the now silent and powerless robots. The whole world fell suddenly into days as gloomy and hopeless as those that marked the early years of the Industrial Revolution. Working days became long and monotonous. Women and children worked twelve hours, men sixteen. Factories became again surrounded by slatternly towns filled with wretched hovels. Buildings that had once been fine homes were turned into workshops where old crones plied their needles.

The Coming of the Water Motor

THE chief sources of power were the waterfalls. Interesting but only partly successful attempts to harness the winds and tides had been made, but the total power derived from these sources was negligible in proportion to that delivered by the waterfalls. In short the outlook for the future of the human race at the beginning of the Eighty-First Century was more gloomy than it had ever been in its history. It was this need, more imperative than any that men had ever experienced, which set scientists and inventors seeking farther and farther afield for fresh reservoirs of power. It was this necessity that finally led to the discovery and application of the water motor.

"The genesis of this invention goes back thousands of years, to the first quarter of the Twentieth when scientists first discovered and studied the cosmic rays. They learned that those rays represented energy radiated through space when atoms of three elements, helium, oxygen or silicon, were spontaneously built up from atoms of hydrogen. A scientist named Millikan was the first to demonstrate this proposition theoretically. He showed that if four atoms of hydrogen, with atomic weights of 1.008, should combine to form one atom of helium, with an atomic weight of 4, energy would be emitted in the process equal to the fractional difference between the weight of four atoms of hydrogen and one atom of helium, or .032.*

"The early scientists, of course, were interested in the problem only from the point of view of explaining the mysterious cosmic rays that they had detected. But our men—when all ordinary sources of energy on Earth had been harnessed, used, and exhausted—turned to it as a means of releasing some of that energy that we knew abounded in earth and air and all the space about us, but which hitherto had defied release by man's ingenuity. They reasoned that in water we had a plentiful, mobile liquid, containing the two elemental gases: oxygen and hydrogen. If, by some means, the hydrogen could be readily separated from the oxygen, and built up into a gaseous element of higher atomic weight, energy would be given off in the process, either in the form of heat or radiation convertible into heat, which could be turned to practical uses.

"I will not say how long they worked on this proposition, or what the preliminary experiments were. The quest was so hopeless that the rich entrepreneurs of the country did not try

---

*Four atoms of hydrogen have total atomic weight of 4.032
One atom of helium has atomic weight of 4.000

to interfere in the tinkerings of these scientists, for they felt no danger to their own position. But one day—it seemed as sudden as that—the problem was solved. A scientist had succeeded in making a metallic alloy containing radioactive elements that had curious properties. Chief among them was this: When a jet of hot water, or steam, was blown upon a plate of it, a violent explosion occurred. At least part of the hydrogen of the water was changed to gas of higher atomic weight, and a portion of the energy given off appeared as heat, causing a sudden expansion, and hence the explosion.

CHAPTER EIGHT
Riotous Days

"IT was a simple matter to incorporate the principle into a motor. A contrivance was built similar to the gasoline engines of former times, with a plate of the new alloy fastened to the inside of the cylinder head. A carburetor passed a spray of heated steam into the cylinder; the moving piston compressed it until, coming in contact with the alloy, the steam exploded. What followed was exactly what had happened in ordinary engines. The power was transmitted through the piston to flywheels and thence to any useful device to which the engine was harnessed. The exhaust gases were let out through a vent.

"The news of the discovery spread over the world almost overnight. Millions of distraught and miserable human beings took new hope. The only men who were not pleased were those who owned the waterfalls. Cloaking themselves with civil authority, they made swift raids on the laboratories, but they were too late. Copies of the magic formula had been broadcast. Plans for the construction of water motors were already in hundreds of hands.

"The first crude motors were, of course, seized as dangerous devices subversive of the public good. Their possession was declared treasonable. But within a year a sufficient number of improved models were in use to break the power of the waterfall magnates. Many of them lost their lives as well as their property in the resulting riots and displays of mob vengeance. Wage earners, too, foreseeing the time when they would be forced from slavery, destroyed machines, factories, and even their masters. A brief period of violence and readjustment followed. Then suddenly the billions of the Earth's people began to realize what so much free power might mean to the cultural development of the race.

"The old benevolent forms of democratic government were revived and adapted to the new conditions of life. The ugly, riverside factories were razed. Every trace of machinery was removed from the world's waterfalls, and they were restored to their original beauty. The race eagerly tried to regain something of the serenity and peace that had marked the golden age of the world before the last Great War. The new power was turned to strictly useful ends, operating mines, ships, and harvesters. Rains from heaven supplied the wants of men. Wage slavery ceased. Slowly, as the population recovered from the deep wounds of the horrible forty-six-year war, quiet and plenty returned. Every man became a little god upon the Earth.

"Sages declared that the millennium had come. Released from his round of ceaseless toil for material ends, every person sought to spend his leisure time improving his mind. Literature, the theatre, music—all the arts, in fact, thrived as never before. It was even in retrospect, a kindly and beautiful time, yet one in which the seeds of destruction were subtly and inevitably growing. Evil roots were working deep into the human consciousness, preparing to burst into sinister flower and to bear the bitter fruits of the coming years.

"As I, the last landed patriarch of this race, write this, I am moved with both compassion and bitterness toward our forefathers, particularly the leaders who did not see the coming disaster. It is now only a little more than nine hundred years since the water motor was perfected and its use made widespread. It seems unbelievable that, in the span of only thirty generations, man should consume all the oceans, the seas and lakes and rivers, and even the surplus moisture of the air. Yet he did this, and in so doing he almost depopulated the globe, destroyed plants, birds, and beasts, and reduced the remainder of the race to misery and slow death.

"The change from quiet to activity was not long delayed. Men suddenly grew weary of bending their enormous new power only to usefulness. It seemed too that the taste for cultural pursuits was abruptly sated. Beauty lay on every hand, and was spurned as common and unexciting. The first evidence of the change began early in the era of peace. Groups of earth-weary men began to wonder how it would be to explore the mysteries of space. Such an abundance of free power made this age-old dream a possibility if some way could be found to concentrate the power for use in rockets. At length one inventor devised a method by which this could be done. Using the power from great quantities of water to turn his generators, he succeeded in electrically manufacturing a concentrated fuel, which, he calculated, would propel him to the moon.

"The uses of peace had not greatly affected the Earth's water supply. It was even argued by some that this supply would never be diminished. Accordingly, there was no popular clamor for the conservation of water when several huge space rockets were constructed, all of them enormously destructive of power. The whole world focused its attention on the first attempts to explore the universe. As everyone soon learned, it was not as simple as had been expected. The designer of the first rocket was blown to bits before he left the Earth. Two others rose from the surface, only to fail before they had gone beyond the sphere of the Earth's gravitational influence. They were drawn back to Earth, and killed in the final plunge.

"Nine attempts were made before one rocket, carrying a party of three men, was successful. It reached the moon, and came away with a report that the satellite was, as had long been supposed, nothing but a dry, lifeless cinder. The success

of the perilous trip, however, fired the imagination of all the
people. If the moon could be reached, it was argued, why not
the other planets? Why not, in fact, the distant suns of outer
space? Almost as if by signal, the world became turbulent,
emotional. Men were no longer content. The boundless
energy of the human spirit, released from the constant toil
that had formerly been necessary to keep it alive, now sought
other means of expression. The pursuit of culture and quiet
refinement was not enough. Action was demanded: danger,
thrills, excitement. A year after the trip to the moon, a
successful voyage was made in a larger space car to the planet
Mars. Ten years later another car reached Venus.

"Now it seemed that at last man was master of the
universe. These successes, productive as they were of
unlimited new knowledge, whetted the appetite of the race
for ventures farther afield. At length two expeditions set out
simultaneously on the long journey to Jupiter, which lies
more than 400,000,000 miles from the sun. It was a breath-
taking attempt: one doomed at the outset to almost certain
failure. The most powerful telescopes on Earth and the most
highly sensitive radio devices were commandeered to keep
track of those intrepid travelers throughout their flight
through the bleakness and cold of outer space.

Into Space

"ONE of the rockets was lost sight of soon after it left our
planet, and was never heard of again. The other, a tiny speck
of burnished metal with its precious cargo of human beings,
flew straight to its mark, and arrived at length upon the
largest of Jupiter's moons. Long before, however, the rocket
had penetrated far beyond the reach of Earthly telescope or
radio. For months we were devoured with impatience and
curiosity, we wondered what our explorers had found at the

157

end of their journey, whether indeed they were still alive, and if so, what had become of them.

"It was only upon their attempted return that we again caught sight of them. Their ether radio signals* caught our attention long before any telescope could be expected to catch sight of them. Something had gone wrong. Through a miscalculation, they were being drawn into the sun!

"Fragmentary messages began coming through to us. 'On the moons of Jupiter we found human beings as intelligent as ourselves—' Then the calls became frantic, incoherent. 'We were forced to leave. We had no time to make our calculations. We have lost our way—' There followed appeals for help—help that no man could give them. They described the flaming surface of the sun as they drew close to destruction. The forces of nature were inexorable; there was no escape. At last they resigned themselves and tried to tell us as much as possible in their final hours of the races they had found. But the electrical interruptions due to the sun's influence were too great. We heard only part of what they said. But we heard enough to cause fresh excitement among the people of the Earth.

"If there were intelligent beings on Jupiter or her satellites, it was argued, they would be as interested in us as we were in them. Then there arose great speculation as to whether the secret of the water-motor and the rocket fuel had been revealed to the Jovians by the voyagers. If so, it was concluded, the application of these principles by the Jovians might bring them upon us for a return visit. It was apparent that our emissaries had been forced to leave Jupiter in haste, perhaps in the face of open hostility. In that case, if the

---

* The ether radio capable of penetrating the Heaviside Layer that had defied the ancients of the 20th to the 25th centuries was devised by Bartlett Graham in 2512.

Jovians actually did visit us, would it be for peaceful purposes, or for conquest?

"So ready were our people for fresh excitement that the idea of resisting an imagined visit of the Jovians took instant hold. It was widely reported that the radio messages from the voyagers were said to have been translated to reveal a threat of invasion. There was tremendous popular clamor for the construction of great engines of defense in case of war. With nothing more than a rumor to go on, our people began to prepare themselves for the battle of the worlds.

"The continents became armed forts. Terrific new explosives, some based on a refinement of the explosion principle of the water motor, others like the rocket fuel, and some still more powerful, were devised. Aircraft capable of transporting garrisons as large as cities were developed and held in readiness. Observatories were erected on every promising point. At length those who at first had been terribly frightened by the prospect of an attack from space now looked forward to it. They were impatient for it to begin, if for nothing more than the spectacle it would afford.

CHAPTER NINE
The Disintegration

"NEEDLESS to say, the Jovians did not attack us.

But the armaments created to defend the Earth from them did not lie idle for many months. There was too much turmoil; too much excitement and quick temper in the air to permit that. As we look back upon it now, knowing as we do what was happening to the atmosphere they breathed, the violent and facile emotions of those men are understandable. But in their own day the events to come were not foreseen, and no one undertook to interpret the new expressions of human temperament as mere matters of chemistry. It was assumed then, as it had been assumed by the bulk of mankind since the beginning of history, that men were being swayed only by their reason, and not by the external world.

"It is difficult to say when or how the last great war was begun in which the human race was to take part. But it started suddenly. Like a spark applied to power, it set the whole world ablaze overnight. The peoples of the Earth, armed to the hilt for an attack from without which did not materialize, seemed ready, and even glad at the suggestion to turn their weapons upon each other. Hemisphere against hemisphere, the planet was suddenly rocked with war in its cruelest and most scientific aspect.

"And as might be supposed the heart of the conflict was the heretofore commonplace and despised water. Water furnished power for the marauding aircraft; water made possible the manufacture of explosives; water afforded energy for all construction, and for destruction as well.

"When a few wise men in both hemispheres pointed to the tremendous use of water as fuel and predicted a drying up of our water supplies they were laughed down or found themselves in their own land accused of treason. Inventors devised ways of using water directly from the oceans, depriving it cheaply of its salt and providing plentiful supplies of fuel for the numberless engines. Military leaders pooh-poohed all suggestions of alarm. If the water were all used up, which was absurd, they said, scientists would find ways of creating more of it synthetically. Or if this proved too difficult, they would find substitutes. What were scientists for, if not to find substitutes for the natural resources mankind had consistently destroyed?

"It must be said, in defense of this view, that not even the wildest dreamer could have believed that all the water would really be consumed. Even with the terrific extravagance of war, our supplies would have lasted for countless centuries before an actual water famine was to be thought of. The amount of water at the beginning of the conflict was so great that had all the land been depressed, so that the oceans were of even thickness over the entire globe, the depth of the universal ocean thus produced would have exceeded a mile.

"What did alarm the chemists, however, was the effect that the water motors were having upon the atmosphere. For the first time since the invention of the alloy, the exhaust gases were carefully analyzed. Many physicists and chemists arrived simultaneously at the conclusion that the power of the machines was due to the fact that in them hydrogen was being built up, not into helium, as had been supposed at first, but into nitrogen. Each fourteen atoms of hydrogen in the water with an atomic weight of 1.008 each, were uniting to form one atom of nitrogen with an atomic weight of 14.008. The energy given off was equal to the difference between the total mass of the hydrogen, or 14.112 and the atomic weight of the nitrogen, 14.008. This large difference was 104, or more than a tenth of the energy in a single hydrogen atom. Naturally, a great part of this force was lost in emanations;

only that which appeared directly as heat was converted into power in the motors.

"But it was not the power phase of the problem that troubled the physicists and chemists. It was the matter of the exhaust gases. Since the air in the beginning was largely made up of nitrogen and oxygen, in proportions of about four to one, the addition of fresh supplies of these two gases seemed at first thought to be unimportant. But while the *identity* of the gases in the air remained virtually the same, the *proportion* was rapidly changing. The exhaust from the motors, it will be observed, was one part nitrogen to seven of oxygen (the change following the disintegration*); also the addition of the exhaust gases rapidly increased the proportion of oxygen to that of nitrogen.

"This discovery, needless to say, was startling in its import and explained many things, including the changes in the atmosphere, the failure of chemists to discover supplies of hydrogen with which to create new oceans of water, the unheard of virulence with which the air was found to attack virtually all exposed metals, and the increasing pressure of the atmosphere. The queer giddiness and excitability of men became understandable, as well as the nutritive changes, numberless hitherto-unexplained deaths (from what had seemed exhaustion and overwork) and the general shortness of life.

"It will be observed from the formula that only a small portion of the mass or weight of the water was lost in the process of transmutation. Consequently the weight of the water, which had formerly pressed only upon the Earth, now

---

* 7 H_2O (in the presence of the alloy)= H_{14} + O_7 =N +70+energy represented by .104 of an H atom. The proportion of nitrogen in normal air is four parts to one of oxygen.

rested, as it were, on the shoulders of men and animals. The concentration of oxygen was becoming so great that iron, copper, brass, tine and many other metals and alloys, if exposed, were sometimes reduced to oxides in a few hours. Breathed into normal lungs the oxygen so concentrated was taken into the blood and the physical effects were similar to that which accompanies the artificial use of oxygen in pulmonary treatments.

A New Race

"ANOTHER effect of the changing climate was the darkening of men's skins. The relatively cloudless skies had permitted the sun to beat down unmercifully upon the Earth. The drying up of the shallower parts of the oceans had covered important portions of the Earth with glittering salt. The glare in some regions was almost unbearable. When nature stepped in, her protective coloration produced at first chagrin and embarrassment, for it had been held a mark of inferiority to be dark-skinned. But men soon began to see that to be dark was advantageous, and the color became so popular that its coming was hastened and exaggerated by artificial stimulation and cosmetics. I do not know whether it was hastened also by the chemical content of the air, or the presence of the unused and little understood emanations from the water motors. But I do know that it came with incredible swiftness, so that in four or five generations the change from light to dark was almost as great as if the blood of a black race had been strongly fused with our own.

"While this was going on, the shortage of water upon the continents was becoming acute. Farmers were no longer able to grow crops for food. The chemists, unable to remedy the lack of moisture or to control the behavior of the weather, came to the rescue in another way. They developed concentrated synthetic foods, thus releasing hundreds of thousands of men from the industries for the pan-hemispheric war. This struggle had entered a new and more bitter phase. The populations of the Earth, realizing for the first time, it seemed, that their fuel supply was slowly diminishing, ceased fighting for the control of land and fought instead for the control of the world's water.

"The races of the Eastern Hemisphere had been most successful in the fight. They already controlled the Indian Ocean, the Mediterranean, the Atlantic, and most of the South Polar Sea. They had encroached along the shoreline of the Pacific on the Chinese side and had gained a foothold on the Pacific in South America. So furious had been the conflicts for these victories that the contents of the oceans had actually been reduced already by nearly a fiftieth of the original amount. The air was deadly with oxygen. The pressure was terrific. Many persons began wearing specially constructed masks to protect themselves from the frightful burning of the air. Others seemed to develop a partial immunity to it, though everyone felt, in some way or other, the effects of the changes that had been made in the vital balance of the elements.

"In addition to these new hazards, including the perils of war, famine, and disease, we were now beset by terrifying movements in the Earth under our feet. The changing pressures caused by the emptying of the ocean beds were bringing about drastic redistributions of the Earth's crust. Yawning chasms opened on the continents. Volcanoes spewed out their fire and destruction upon many lands. The seas often trembled with the violence of movements going on underneath. Rushing into fissures, the waters sometimes met eternal fires deep in the Earth, and came back to the surface in clouds of explosive steam. Great quantities of it soaked downward also into new caverns in the interior of the globe, and so were lost to us.

"Moved by these evidences of destruction in inanimate things, our people became like madmen. It is difficult to describe the extravagances to which they went to carry on their petty war. At one time soldiers of our race drove tunnels thirty miles underground to blast an enemy city.

The enemy retorted in kind, sending upon us such a rain of aerial torpedoes that we were at a loss to know whether it was more dangerous to let them fly or shoot them down. At the expense of great quantities of power, we erected batteries that would hurl projectiles a distance of two hundred miles into the enemy camp. They protected themselves with a veritable barrage of electrical energy, laid down curtain-like around their works, and generated at the expense of almost incalculable power. It was the desire of both sides to make it a war to end all wars. It was hoped that it could be brought to a conclusion before all the water of the globe had been exhausted.

CHAPTER TEN
A Crisis

"THIS was the condition of the Earth and of mankind four hundred years ago. Each side vied with her to produce some more daring, more diabolical, or more wasteful engine of destruction or defense. Nevertheless, so great was the total quantity of water in proportion to the inventiveness of men, that even then the world might have been saved. If the war had been stopped four hundred years ago our children today might be playing in grassy meadows by the margins of silvery lakes. Birds might still be thronging the air and airships would fly serenely over the remnants of our once billowing seas.

"But in the year 8522 occurred the worst catastrophe of all. An inventor, of the Caucasian race,* experimenting in his laboratory, came upon a method whereby the catalytic alloy of the water motors** could be finely divided and scattered in water, producing in this form the familiar explosion without the aid of carburetor or initial heat. He took his discovery to the War Department, with the suggestion that the metal be scattered into the oceans, thereby setting them by spontaneous dissolution into fields of flame and vapor. Our people, perceiving that in this they had found a way of conquering the enemy at a single stroke, yielded to his counsel. They dammed off great bodies of water for their own use, throwing huge dykes across the necks of estuaries and gulfs in our control. Into the remainder, which included all that part of the sea and the ice of the North and South Poles that touched upon the shorelines held by the Asiatics, they cast great quantities of the powder.

---

* Rabo Collum IV   ** Known as pergnium

"No sooner had they done this than the waters burst into flame like lakes of burning oil. Upheavals rent the air and caused the land to shake. The alloy settled through the layers of the deep. Far down beneath the waves the liquid began to disintegrate. The ice at the poles melted from the terrific heat. A frightful furnace covered half the world.

"The inventor who had planned this holocaust had calculated rightly. The burning of the seas did kill the Asiatics in their cities. Those who hurried inward to escape the burning waters starved in the desert lands. They were unable to come at us across the miles of flaming ocean. I am ashamed to say also that for three weeks, while the oceans burned, my people gave themselves up to the most disgusting orgies of celebration. The author of this incredible horror was feted as if he were a benefactor of the race; he was enthroned like Nero, and like that bestial emperor he sang and played while half the world burned. But for three weeks only did the celebration last.

"At the end of that time the bones of millions of Asiatics were bleaching on the glittering sides of the salt dunes they had once held. The waters that had lapped those shores, had disappeared in heat and gases—to return no more.

"But something else had happened also—a circumstance which remains more or less inexplicable to this day. By some unforeseen means, a great quantity of the destroying alloy had found its way from the boiling oceans into our own private seas. Perhaps the explosions of the deep had cast the metal like fine, impalpable dust into the air, and it had settled again of its own accord in the water that had been reserved from the conflagration for the use of the Western race. In any case, the boiling and explosions of the waters spread over the globe like a loathsome epidemic, mysterious and unpreventable.

"One day a body of water would be lying still, with only the twinkle of the bright sun upon its wavelets and the sedgy grasses growing luxuriantly around the edge; the next, it would be covered with the boiling vapors of dissolution. Within a week the explosions would rock it to the depths; the heat would drive all persons living nearby from their homes. In a month the basin would be dry, a mocking glitter of salt.

"It was horrible, horrible! For a few weeks, suffering humanity, or that remnant of it which was left, beheld in wondering silence the spread of this terror over the remaining habitable portions of the globe. Then there was questioning. Scientists were importuned for aid. Rioting broke out in cities, and savagery took the place of feasts and celebration. One by one the large bodies of water, which had been reserved for use after the death of the last Asiatic, now disappeared. People, in great numbers, began to die of thirst upon the salty deserts of their own making. The inventor, who three months before, had been feted like a king, suddenly found himself caught by a mob, and when he confessed that he had no magic whereby he could destroy the Frankenstein monster he had created, they put him to death by horrible torture.

"Still the terror spread. The number of human beings dwindled day by day. Animals, birds, insects, and all manner of crawling, running, or flying things disappeared. It was as if the avenging hand of God were wiping the old Earth clean again and clothing her afresh with a vegetation of brilliant solar salt, the glitter of which destroyed the eyes.

"At last the survivors, numbering twenty thousand, reached this valley at the bottom of the ocean, a valley surrounded by high furrows which had once been mountain chains beneath the waves. By some miracle, the water here had been saved. It sparkled cheerfully in this, our last stronghold. Welcome plants were growing around the lake's broad edges. The valley was a fairyland, a premise of renewed life. All the race might gather here and create a new civilization.

CHAPTER ELEVEN
Feverish Activity

"THE rulers of the little band which settled here in 8740 were wise. They forbade from the start the unlimited use of water-motors. All but a necessary few of these engines were destroyed. The fluid of life was to be carefully husbanded. A new city of stone was to be built for all eternity beside the quiet shore—a city practically without metal, for virtually no known metal except the disintegrating alloy could endure the extremely high concentration of oxygen in the air.

"Stone, fortunately, was plentiful, and soon the city began to grow. Among this little band, the terror of total extinction was forgotten. On the placid lake there was no sign of the vapor or the explosions that had burned out the rest of the world. Men who had seen lakes, equally quiet, suddenly burst into unexplained activity, now glanced at this lake daily with the assurance that here no dissolution would come. Normal evaporation took place, of course, and there were other losses. But they were compensated partly by little rainstorms, which, from time to time, returned part of the water the sun had removed. The pool was salty; at its edges the crusted crystals made a shining rim. But salt did not trouble us greatly, for methods had long been known by which it could be cheaply removed.

"But however carefully it was watched, the level of the pool began to slowly go down. It was apparent that we were gradually using up our water, losing it by evaporation and by seepage into the Earth. The life of the city moved in upon the lake as it became smaller and smaller. The outer buildings were deserted progressively in favor of those closer to the cooling beach.

"The dry Earth was almost windless, but there was, nevertheless, a constant fluttering of the air around the edges of our valley. On the wings of this breeze the higher surfaces began to shower us day and night with storms of sand. We reasoned that the presence of the moisture in our valley, when all the rest of the globe was dry and hot, set up atmospheric disturbances that brought the wind.

"Corps of sand-shovelers were therefore organized early in the life of the community to keep the streets and areaways clear. But from the first, many people despaired of ever keeping back the floods of quartz and salt, which drifted ceaselessly over the cliffs upon our roofs.

"Another intense activity in the city was connected with chemical research. In one of the tallest buildings of the settlement it went on continuously, even feverishly. Our scientists, faced by the direst necessity, were seeking some secret from the elements that would enable us to restore the oceans, lakes, rivers, and meadows.

"But the secret was destined never to be discovered. In a few years every method possible to us had soon exhausted. Meanwhile, other difficulties began to arise. Necessity, instead of bringing the members of the little colony closer together in a wise struggle against nature, seemed to provoke internal quarrels. Disease became common and was difficult to check. So careful were we in using our wretched supply of water that often the necessities of sanitation were neglected. The concentrated, synthetic foods upon which we were trying to exist had begun to have their effect; bodies which could live on them for a long time when they were supplemented by natural foods from time to time, now began to go to pieces under the necessity of eating laboratory preparations and nothing else. And so the little community went on year after year, fighting its losing battle against inexorable nature.

"And then, in 8830, it happened. A watchman came hurrying one morning to the governor of the city with the news that the catalyst in some way had gotten into the lake.

"Looking out at sunrise he had beheld the familiar boiling in the water. Vapor was rising at a spot near its center. When, or how, or from what source that accursed bit of metal had come we could not tell; but as they gathered, the few hundreds of them, at the shore of the lake they all saw that the watchman had been right. The lake was indeed in the toils of the accursed metal. It appeared that the amount of material causing the disturbance was small; dissolution at this rate would take years. But it would, nevertheless, go on until the last drops of our precious liquid were gone, until we were left to die in agonies of thirst on the lifeless desert.

"Straight up over the center of the lake rose the vapor and expanded gas. It was faintly visible, like a thin wavering plume of incense. At its base the water boiled and rumbled, sending up huge bubbles, which burst to discharge their gases out into the air. Our people cried out in despair when they saw what was going on. 'This is the end,' declared one man solemnly. 'This day we behold our doom, for nothing can save our water now!'

" 'But see here,' exclaimed another, 'the amount of metal in the lake is small. Perhaps it is only a single grain, like dust. Why not let a diver enter the lake to see if he can reach it and bring it out?'

"This insane plan took hold of popular fancy immediately, though reason would have told any of the volunteers that they could never succeed. The water in the vicinity of the metal was boiling hot, the whole lake filled with terrible explosions. In addition, the metal hurled here and there by the violence of the disintegration of water, was skipping like a demon beneath the surface of the lake. It would be practically impossible for a diver to get it or hold it—and furthermore, the explosions would burn him up in an instant.

Madness

"THESE things were quickly pointed out by the sane ones present. But the terror of the people had already produced an enthusiasm for the insane plan. No less than ten young men came forward to offer themselves. At first only one was sent down, in a diving suit, to try his luck. He never came back to the surface. Later ten went at once, to see if by their combined efforts they could not succeed where one alone had failed. Fifteen minutes later the maimed bodies of some of them, horribly burned, were thrown to the surface. The others were never found.

"Fully a hundred of our bravest men were lost in subsequent mad attempts to remove the destroyer in the basin's bottom. It seems to me now to have been simply an orgy for self-destruction. Every attempt ended in failure. The inhabitants of the valley were again frenzied with alarm. It was suggested that heavy boats be built to move over the seat of the disturbance, letting down buckets to catch the offending metal and lift it to the top. One man went so far as to fashion a crude diving bell, in which he went down to the bottom to study the situation. When the apparatus was hauled out again he was quite dead, his body disintegrated by the intense heat.

"What appeared to be the most practical scheme was proposed by a man who had formerly been a leader of one of the gangs of sand-shovelers. He suggested that a long trench be dug at one side of the lake, and that artificial currents be set up in the water to sweep the alloy into this where it could be bottled up with a dam of sand. In practice, however, this plan met with insurmountable difficulties. Such frightful currents were already being set up in the lake by the presence of the catalyst that our own puny efforts only added to the general confusion. When we had finished digging the trench we tried unsuccessfully for weeks upon weeks to induce the alloy to float into it. The thing behaved as cannily as though it had been alive, as if it were consciously avoiding being entrapped.

"When we had wasted two or three months in these futile and distinctly costly efforts, we became convinced that nothing in our power would stop the dissolution of the lake. A horrible calm then settled over the valley. At times hysterical, then silent and morose, the people resigned themselves to the end. Sand-shoveling was given up. The encroaching dust year after year was covering house after house at the outskirts of the city. The inhabitants, no longer animated to resistance, simply moved into empty places nearer the lake, whose level was now dropping at an appreciable rate. It was clear that between the sand and the alloy we had only a few more years of life. There was no hope—unless help should come. That brings us to my own time.

"*Unless help should come!* Almost as if it had sprung spontaneously from our hearts, the idea had taken hold of many persons that aid might indeed be summoned—from some other planet. Our desperate minds, wandering through the possibilities, returned again and again to those beings whom explorers had discovered upon far-off Jupiter. What kind of men were they? Once they had filled us with dread and alarm. Now they were thought of as omniscient and kindly creatures, ready at an instant to succor such hopeless folk as we. A project was rapidly developed to signal into space by radio and beacon, telling any chance listeners of our distress and urging them to come to the rescue. Of course we realized that only a chance of a billion to one would bring the message to the ears of anyone who understood our language. But we felt that beings from outside becoming aware that sentient Earthlings existed would be prompted to come and investigate.

"It was no longer a question of saving the Earth. It was a question of preserving the race, on whatever planet or in whatever condition was possible. As the remnant of a race which had once been so proud—we were humble enough now!

"Our efforts to remove the alloy had resulted in carrying it to the farther end of the lake, where the water was deepest. We chose the quiet part for the erection of our signal tower, because we felt that spot would remain free longest from the drifting sand. Out of the mountain at the valley's eastern side we quarried glossy milk-colored stone. Experts with the chisel cut and shaped it, and at length we erected a tower that was both a monument and a signal station. We assembled in it the best available machinery for radio communication, using the highest-powered ether radio that we could build. When everything was ready, we set up water motors once more, and drew from our scanty water supply the power we needed.

"At the time the first of our messages went out to the universe* there were fewer than 150 human beings still living in the colony. The others had, in the years of our occupation, died of disease, accident, toil or premature old age brought on by the too-rich atmosphere. Hardly any of us was free from some malady or other engendered by the nature of our life. There were, in all, forty-three families, and our social system, like our physical constitutions, had fallen into a state of virtual collapse. At the time we had a man who, out of habit,

---

* 8916

was called the governor: he had received the office by an election in which few had been interested. He had no means at enforcing his commands; the work of the community was done through mutual willingness—no more. We existed in short, in a state of amiable anarchy, a condition of which poets once sang. But we would gladly have traded all the heavenly delights of such an association for despotism, had it meant plenty of water to drink, foods grown upon land, and the meat or animals.

Dark Days

"I WAS at the time sixty-six years old—a very old man as such things were reckoned. My daughter Nina was eighteen, my son Nino a year younger. My wife had died two years earlier of heart trouble brought on by the oxygen concentration. Ours was an average family, in numbers and ages. There were hardly ever any new births. Why this should be I do not know; it appeared that even the biological verities were deserting us, that our women were sterile and our men hopelessly weak and short-lived. Even had our water remained untouched by the curse, I doubt if we could have been able to keep our wretched race going much longer.

"Day after day, night after night, we sent the messages out, supplemented by light signals in every language and code we knew. But no answer came. As time passed, it became increasingly clear that no answer would come.

"Gradually we resigned ourselves to the inevitable. There was a suggestion on the part of some that we appoint a day for prayers and forgiveness, and by others a day of abandon and rejoicing, at the end of which we would all drown ourselves in the little pool of water that was left, surfeiting ourselves for once in the cool wetness of it. Of course, the sane ones among us hastily vetoed this plan. Two general councils of the colony were called to discuss what should be done, but both broke up with disagreements and bad feeling. All were oppressed by the hopelessness of continuing our resistance; yet most of us shrank from a violent end.

"This feeling was intensified when the members of two families formed a suicide pact and actually killed themselves by cutting the veins of their wrists. The horror that attended the discovery of this deed, more effectively than any exhortation, turned the rest of us from the thought of suicide. The community went into a state of religious frenzy thereafter for several days. One young fellow who set himself up as our spiritual leader held a series of "revival" meetings in the great hall of the town. Aided by the twin compulsions of fear and hysteria, he was singularly successful in producing unusual results among his congregation.

"I mention these things because they are indicative of our state of mind at that time. We were in the darkness that is said of the affairs of men to precede the dawn of a new day. Baffled in all our efforts for survival we had given in to the inevitable, relieving our despair with such nostrums as were at hand. Religion was one of these. Another was aimless toil of such a nature that it robbed the mind of opportunity for activity. One of these occupations was the building of a giant pedestal that should for a long time rise above the encroaching sand. The idea was started by one of the artistic members of the community with an idea of asserting some dominance over nature. As this man explained his idea in its ramifications it took hold of the imagination of our little band and we set to work with a will to put it into execution. What we were to do was to erect a great stone pedestal that should tower above all the other buildings. At its top we set a statue of a man and in his hand we placed a cylinder of the non-rusting metal alloy, to contain a history of our race. To me was given the task of writing that history. We still hoped that rescue would come from the heavens. Therefore we arranged it so that if any of us were still alive, the removal of the cylinder would set in motion machinery that would cause the statue to disappear through the base. But if we were all gone, there would be no reaction and the black figure of a man would remain for all times atop our milky shaft, a monument to a dead and forgotten race.

"In the building of this monument to the race the few members of the colony sought relief. Rapidly it grew to completion. Nino, my son, every day took his pick and bar and walked to the quarries, where he, with others, delighted in hand-working the stone during the daylight hours. Heaven knows what he expected to gain by such primitive toil. He pursued his labors quietly, in moody silence. Whether there was in them the working of a blind instinct I do not know; but it was through them the cavern was discovered and new hope stirred in the colony.

CHAPTER TWELVE
Water!

"I SHALL never forget the day when he came racing over the flat, sandy bottom of the valley to us, shouting the news that his pick had burst through the rock and that an empty space was beneath it. He stopped two or three men on the way, gesticulating, trying to explain, but they only smiled and turned away indifferently. Insanity taking many forms had become common among us. They marked Nino down as another case of dementia. But at length he came to me, so out of breath that he could hardly talk.

" 'My pick broke through,' " he said, " 'Water—water—under the mountain!' "

"Alas for our human incredulity! At first I looked at him as the others had. I hurried him into our house and made him lie down.

" 'I'm not crazy,' " he insisted. " 'I saw it. A cavern under the mountain. And in it there is a lake of water, and from the ceiling there comes a kind of chemical light!' "

"He went on, piling up such details, until I could not but be convinced. I called on the governor and laid the facts before him. It could do no harm to investigate, I said, and if there really were a cavern as the boy had said, it might mean the saving of all of us.

"At length he agreed, and two men were sent to investigate. They were gone less than an hour, and when they returned they reported that there was actually such a cavern. It was like hearing a reprieve. A great body of fresh water, untouched by the burning metal!

"The governor immediately called us together on the beach of our boiling sea. All came except those who were so overcome by disease that they could not leave their beds. A sorry lot we were. Many were haggard and emaciated, worn with worry and dread. Others had been crippled by work in the quarries, and clad in tattered garments stood upon makeshift crutches. All of us were undernourished. Even the strong bodies of the young folk, including those of my son and daughter, who had both insisted upon working in the open air, showed the horrible effects of our strange life.

" 'A great cavern has been discovered—' said the governor quietly, motioning with his arm toward the mountain range across the lake. 'It may mean life for us!' There was a catch in his voice; for a moment he could not go on.

"At this pronouncement, the members of the crowd appeared to be stricken dumb. There was no shouting, no sobbing, no hysterical weeping, as I had expected. Somebody mumbled a prayer; I could not tell who it was. As they stood there, two men slipped to the ground, overcome by weakness and disease. The meaning of the governor's words at last penetrated the crowd. They moved suddenly, like a band of sheep, toward the mountain.

"A few strong men made a larger hole in the rock with their picks, and stared down into the blackness below. There, surely, was water; and from above rolled a heatless flame which supported and made possible a strange and ghastly vegetable life. It was a life unknown on the surface of the Earth, life that had developed in this underground cavern away from the sun.

"All crowded close to view the wonder. Many were for letting themselves down immediately into the opening and plunging their weary bodies into the cool lake. But the governor restrained them.

" 'It is our last body of water,' he declared. 'So far the mineral which has destroyed all the rest has not reached here. *We must not let the outer air get at this lake.* Instead let us tunnel under the ground and enter the cavern from its own level.

We must screen and filter the air we let in and guard in every way the precious moisture.'

"Aghast at the prospect of so much work, but never the less obedient, the crowd fell back. Stones were rolled over the jagged opening Nino had made.

"Then began the cruelest period of all. Weak, worn and hopeless all they were, my people threw themselves into that frightful labor, digging tunnels both from the largest building of our stone city of Mansende to the cavern, and from the bottom of the hollow signal tower we had erected in the drying lake. Before we started, a chemist was lowered into the cave by ropes, to test the vegetation there. He reported that the water was sweet and good, and that in it was a species of bloated fish, that would help sustain life. Further, he reported, the vegetation would supply us with a kind of pulpy food as well as fuel.

"The flame of hope again leaped high in human breasts when the work began. Deep under the hollow milky tower we sank a shaft, and under Mansende another. And from these shafts level tunnels converged upon a spot we had selected to serve as an entrance to the cavern. It was slow, terribly exhausting work, accomplished only by brute force with little aid from machinery. We no longer had machines. The art of working metals, thanks to the corroding atmosphere, had virtually disappeared. We were reduced to the implements of the stone age as we burrowed like moles under the ground. The work day and night went on in weary shifts.

"Man after man died at his toil. Still the rest kept on, without a murmur, without a protest. For it was not themselves they were working for, but for posterity. No man insufficiently nourished, with only half enough water, struggling with blunt tools and archaic methods, would ever sacrifice himself for his own life alone as these men did. He would rather die in torment than stand the torture of the shafts and tunnels. Yet the members of the colony did it, realizing, many of them, that they would never live to see the completion of the task.

"I was often a sharp critic of my people, speaking of their narrowness, their tendency to quarrel over nothing, to fight and kill without provocation, to be petty and childish in their relations with each other and with the world. But I had cause to be proud of them on those last terrible days. With the desperation of both hope and hopelessness, they drove those tunnels to completion! It was as if, in that final great attempt, they had tried to atone for the destruction they had wrought on the ancient Earth, for the cruelty and wantonness of their wars and the wastage in earlier years. With an eye only to preserving their race, not themselves, they fought against death itself to make a habitation in which the coming generation could continue life.

"And in view of this tremendous sacrifice, what happened seemed like a cruel, merciless jest of fate.

The Nemesis

"WHEN the tunnels had been completed, one linked the cavern underground with our signal tower from which every day the desperate appeals still went forth into the heavens for aid. Another linked it with the fast-disappearing city of Mansende, which we had planned to abandon as soon as the underground works were ready, and a third with the bottom of the tower on which the statue had been erected. The creeping sand by that time had covered nearly all the outlying building! As a result it had become the custom of our women, only thirty-eight in number, to band together in one large stone building for mutual companionship while their men were at work.

"It happened on the day that the huge air-filters were being installed to keep the atmosphere of the cavern clear of the destroying alloy. All the men of the settlement, except a few who were too ill to help, had been called out to assist in the construction of these filters. In addition, Nina, wearing the attire of a man, and insisting that she was as able to take a man's part in the work, was with us.

"A sufficient supply of power for our final operations was of the greatest importance and it had been decided to set up additional water-motors. These machines had lain for a long time unused and their condition was none too good. Furthermore, we had no expert engineers left to inspect them for us. The men chosen to tend them were selected not for their knowledge of mechanics, but simply because of their unfitness to do other tasks. It is to these circumstances that I attribute the disaster that occurred, though of course I do not know, and no one will ever know, what really happened.

"It was about three o'clock in the afternoon. Nino, myself, and two or three others, including Nina, were working on the farther side of the lake beyond the signal tower, when without warning we were thrown from our feet by a terrific explosion. I remember thinking at first that it was an earthquake, for the shaking of the earth was similar to the trembling of the earth that the race had experienced following the disappearance of the oceans and the subsequent readjustment of the continental levels. My next thought was that the stone walls of the mountain had given way and the cavern fallen in. But it was neither. There had been a frightful explosion in the vicinity of the water-motors. The whole battery of them had been blown up as cleanly as a bubble is pricked.

"The roar of the explosion and its echoes were still ringing in my ears as I rose to my feet and staggered about to give aid to my companions. Barely able to walk, we decided that the first thing to do was to take account, to see how many had been killed by the explosion. We numbered the men who were still visible, and learned that twenty-one had been killed outright. Several had disappeared in the blast; the others were mangled, dead, or dying. Only a scant dozen, counting myself, Nino and Nina, were left. All of us were dazed, stricken by the double shock of the concussion and the knowledge of what had happened to our companions.

"When we had assembled the living and done what we could for those about to die, we turned toward Mansende. Our hearts were weary, already too used to suffering to be much further moved by a new pain. Nevertheless, when we had proceeded about half of the distance from the shore of the sea to the nearest buildings I heard a hoarse cry. The man ahead of me darted into a shambling run, waving his arms. Then we all perceived what had happened. The huge hall where our women were kept had tumbled in under the combined pressure of the sand and the decoy of the rotten stone and mortar. Just as in the days long past, a shout was sometimes sufficient to loosen a frightful snow slide on the mountains, so had the blast in the valley been sufficient to precipitate the crumbling of the hall, which might otherwise have stood for years.

"Like madmen we hastened to the spot. It was apparent at first glance that there was no use to tear away the stone. Not a sound, not a cry or scream came from that still, crumpled pile. All who had been inside were dead, beyond a doubt: the women, children, and young girls—all except my Nina.

"Then I silently thanked God that I had permitted her to go with us to the work. The other men hurled themselves at the ruins. They were lunatics, crazed at last with grief, horror, and hopelessness. I saw staring madness in their eyes, tortured twisting in the muscles of their faces. I said to Nino and Nina, 'We had better go and leave them for a while with their grief.'

"But already the others had forsaken their struggle with the stones and were staring at us. No longer did they look like the friends and companions I had been working with an hour before.

"Seeing us standing apart, they beheld us suddenly as strangers untouched by the disaster with my whole family still at my side. In their frenzy they saw some evil sign in that. Their crazed minds somehow connected me with the catastrophe that had wiped out their own chances of posterity and made mockery of the toil of months.

"I saw that it was already too late to leave them peacefully. One was pointing at us, gesticulating. He babbled incoherently. His eyes were ablaze with an unreasoned hate. With Nino following in our rear, his pistol drawn to give battle if any of them attacked us, Nina and I hastened to the entrance of the Mansende tunnel, which would take us through to the cavern and safety.

"We reached the door of the building. Nina had already started down the long stairs to the bottom of the shaft. It appeared that we would escape without trouble, but at that moment the madmen lunged into a concerted, insane attack. Shouting and hurling stones, they first sought to grapple with Nino, who was retreating stubbornly toward the portal of the building.

"At the door he drew and leveled his Kappa-pellet pistol* and fired. It was our only chance; they would have killed all three of us had we not taken such desperate measures.

---

* Invented by Partremo in 8012. Fires a pellet of concentrated bulolic acid that eats away human tissue instantly.

And so at the end—with the race almost wiped from the Earth—we were still at the age-old game of men killing men.

"I shudder to relate the gruesome incidents which followed. With stones, clubs, and the deadly pellets we drove them back, but they came on again, now armed themselves. In all my life I have not seen such ferocity, such mad determination to kill. One by one Nino brought them down; he was a strong defender, and he was moved to excesses of heroism by the knowledge that upon his strength and skill depended the lives of his aged father and his young sister.

"In addition, protected as we were, we had the advantage. The battle, it soon became apparent, could have but one outcome.

"THE area outside our door was a shambles. Unable to realize the hopelessness of their attack, or so crazed they did not care, our assailants now remaining threw themselves at us again and again. The wounded and dying, unable to do more than lift a leg or arm, still tried to come at us upon the ground. Upon expiring they cast upon us such glances of hate that I shall dream of them until my dying day.

"After what seemed hours it was over. We were saved.

"But Nino was wounded. Stones and bullets had struck him. He was exhausted by the struggle. Tenderly Nina and I carried him down the stairway and through the long passage to our new home. We gathered up the strange, wild plants about the cavern floor and made him a bed. Food we brought him, and quantities of the abundant sweet water of the ebony lake.

"For many days he lay between life and death. We nursed him continually, cherishing the tiny spark of life. At length he began to heal. Eventually he recovered, though one arm remained stiff and almost useless.

"Now we were faced with the gloom of our new world. The three of us, disheartened, despairing, yet hanging on to life somehow felt that on us depended the prolonging of the race. I confess that we pondered again and again that awful problem which was nameless and unspoken among us, but nevertheless uppermost in all our minds. *How should we reproduce and carry on without committing that which had been thought an unforgettable sin these many thousands years?*

"But I cannot dwell on that now. We are placing this manuscript in the cylinder to await a rescue from space. I am continuing the story, keeping it up to date so that if we die without release from our predicament, a possible visitor may know how we fought to the last.

"Nino has meanwhile fixed the statue so that if you who take this message observe the ebon figure to fall through the crystal tower, and a trapdoor to appear in its place, you will know that someone or other is still living in the depths, crying and praying for rescue at your hands. Please then, open the trap as follows: tap five times smartly on the door. Then wrench it open with the little lever that will appear. You will then find that the descent of the figure has brought up a fibrous ladder from below, down which you may climb to the passageway.

"When the last of us feels that death is near he will set an automatic contrivance that will break the contact of the machine, and seal the tower-top forever against approach. If it be true, Discoverer, that when you take this message from the ebon hand, it move not, then you may be assured that there is nothing living on the Earth; that this cavern is our tomb.

"Then let the death of man be a warning to all the other races of the universe: *that man by science, can aid himself to reach heights unsurpassed; but that by science he can also destroy himself, and is likely to, unless he is guided by wisdom rather than passion.*"

CHAPTER THIRTEEN
Difficulties

THE father of Allus Marce laid down the last sheet of the translation with a trembling hand, and stared across the table at the quiet youth.

"Marce," he said, his voice throbbing a little with the emotion the document had aroused in him. "What did the statue do, when you removed the cylinder?"

"It turned half way around, and disappeared through the tower."

"Then—they are still alive!"

"So I have reasoned!"

The two men were silent for a long time, contemplating this tragedy of a dead world, and the compelling call across space for aid.

"But now—who knows?" ventured the elder. "Perhaps before this they have all died. It takes months as time is measured on Tellus, to make the trip. Nearly a Tellurian year has passed already since you took this message from the statue's hand—"

He went on, musingly, but Marco interrupted impetuously.

"Then there is all the more reason to make a return trip!"

"A return trip?"

"Of course. We must return and rescue them. Think of it, three persons, blood relatives perhaps, suffering there in a cave, waiting for death. And we two are the only ones in the universe who know their plight!"

The head of the house of Altus tapped the tabletop with his long white fingers.

"It appears that you are not aware of the difficulties," he said.

Marce replied with vigor. "Who should know the difficulties better than I? Haven't I already made the journey?"

His father stopped him with a gesture.

"The mechanical difficulties I will concede to you," he said. "It was the political difficulties of which I spoke. Do you not know that Dolmician has forbidden anyone else to leave Pleida and her satellites without the express permission of Salvarius Carde, who is now Minister of Space Exploration. Do you think you could get Salvarius Carde's consent to let you make this trip, even if other details could be arranged? Would it not be somewhat difficult to explain to him how you came by the information here contained?"

The patriarch tapped lightly the Tellurian manuscript. "And if there were a return voyage, do you suppose Salvarius Carde would let you lead it, you who were the youngest of his companions, and the man whom he saw fit to ignore in claiming the glory of the find?"

"But we could go—without his consent."

"That would be a declaration of civil war. The legions of Dolmician would descend upon us in much less than the time it would take you to return from Tellus."

The old man saw the light of battle suddenly leap into the eyes of his son. But he held up his hand to stop him before he could utter a word.

"I know, I know," he said quietly. "It is what we all want—but the satellites are not yet ready for revolution. We are not yet united. We lack a strong young leader whose past exploits have proved him able and worthy to lead the whole group into battle against Dolmician and the despotic Pleidans. We need..." The old man's voice wavered for an instant, "—power. We have at this moment, no weapon as great as any that the Pleidans could bring against us."

"Have there been overtures? Have the other satellites spoken of revolt?"

The patriarch nodded.

"Often," he said. "But I am too old to lead it, and others are afraid."

Marce was silent. His father held his arm and continued, "It is a thing not generally known among our people, Marce, but our engineers have finished a careful survey and have learned the truth. Our satellites have long depended upon their internal heat, generated by chemical changes, to make life possible. Within recent years there has been an alarming diminution of this heat. We are threatened with slavery from Pleida, and with freezing and starvation from the moons on which we live. These are the things which are rapidly bringing our affairs to a head, yet we rulers dare not tell the people for fear it would destroy their courage."

"What our people need," replied Allus Marce after a time, "is an issue—some emotional point of contact upon which they can unite. In addition, before the rebellion could be a success, we need a new source of power to supplement our waning internal fires and to drive our war engines."

The old man nodded, but did not speak. Marce continued:

"I am forming a plan. We will build a space car—secretly—according to methods and designs I know. We will assemble most of the members of the crew that Salvarius Carde took to Tellus with him; they are his enemies and they will work with us. In the meantime, I will quietly acquaint our leaders with the purpose of the rescue voyage to Tellus. We will show them the Tellurian document. The heads of all the satellites will learn of it and keep their counsel.

I Will Lead Them

"WHEN everything is ready we shall take off for Tellus, secretly if possible. The Tellurians have the key to our problem, for with their water-motors we could use our seas to furnish power to use against Pleida. It is common knowledge that there is more water than land on the satellites, while on the planet the reverse is true. Even if they should get hold of our secret, we would have the best of the Pleidans there."

"You are assuming, then, that the Tellurians are still alive?"

"Yes."

"But if they are not?"

"Then there will be nothing left for us but to fight with what weapons and cunning we have. I will lead our people. If they will follow me."

Marce spoke simply, gently, yet with a firmness that was new to him. The head of the House of Allus rose and placed his hands firmly upon the sturdy shoulders of his son.

"Now, Marce, I am proud of you!" he exclaimed. "It is the first time you have spoken like a man. No more a boy now!"

Marce smiled. "But what am I?" he asked. "Pleidan or Tellurian?"

"Neither, and both. In you are mingled the bloods of two great peoples of the solar system, and in you are the combined strengths of those races. You are a fit leader for the war I have so planned and dreamed of—our war of liberation."

"But now as to our rescue trip—"

"It will be dangerous and difficult, building your space flier without Dolmician getting word of it."

"Nevertheless, we must do it. And we must hurry."

"I'll give orders for beginning it at once," said the patriarch. "You will have full charge. God grant your journey will not be in vain!"

CHAPTER FOURTEEN
Fire in the Lake

AN OBSERVER, standing upon the rim of the valley, in the mid-afternoon of this summer's day, would have been struck by a quality of deadness about it, for in it nothing moved. It was a sand-ridden waste, in which the sand had all but wiped out the last traces of man's former presence. The burning sun passed almost directly over the hollow, filling it with an intense, quivering heat. The white valley floor gave back the rays. The air flickered as if protesting against the pressure of the sun.

More than a year and a half had gone by since Allus Marce had alighted on the tower and taken the precious message. The last of the stone buildings of Mansende had crumbled into ruin. In the fast-filling hollow two objects still attested to the fact that men had once been there; the tower, and a jagged wound in the side of the mountain, which formed the valley wall, where the stone had been quarried. The quarry edges were still sharp and clean. Its only defect was a small hole toward the back and near one side, where Nino's pick, bursting through, had exposed the cavern.

So much for the appearance of the valley; an observer would not have long contemplated it unless he was a student of abandoned limekilns or of hellish spots where no form of life could exist. But he would have been struck, had he been standing upon the mountain to the east, by the endless reverberations of the air and ground, sometimes more felt than heard; the sense of an incessant pounding going on under the Earth. They filled the hot basin with their echoes. There was a sense of imminent danger in them, as though the mountain contained a demon who was now springing by his subterranean home.

In addition to the sound there was one more evidence that something under the mountain was amiss. The little pile of rocks, which had once masked the entrance from the quarry to the cavern, had been tumbled slightly aside. From the opening there was now issuing a stream of heated gas. It moved upward silently into the intense, cloudless sky, hardly visible except for the aberrations the heat of it produced in the still air.

Through the cold, illimitable distances of outer space came one ray of sunlight so precisely aimed that it passed through the stream of gas and into the hole, and played on the surface of the waters underneath. Its sparkling reflections made more luminous the natural radiance of the cavern's roof. It disclosed that there were two persons living in the cave, beside the lake.

One was lying on a pallet of herbs and leaves. The spattering sunlight played upon him with a gaiety that mocked the hot air. Nina was sitting beside him on a little tussock of fiber she had made. She, too, was watching the sun, wondering if another afternoon would still find them there or whether, when the distant orb again lighted the cavern, it would sparkle on emptiness, finding the frail moving ferment which had been man gone forever.

For it was clear what had happened to the precious lake. The disintegrating alloy had fallen into it, gaining entrance either through the pick-hole at the edge of the roof, or through one of the unscreened passages. From the nethermost parts of the huge underground room came rumblings and explosions. The roarings were augmented by reverberations, which passed a dozen times across the cavern. Fresh thunders arose, endlessly from the heart of the lake. The shore-line of the pool had drawn together until the lake occupied but half the space it formerly had filled. It was an all-too-evident fact that life in the cavern would soon be as impossible as in the hot dry valley outside.

The old man on the pallet was dying. His eyes, half-open, were content to follow listlessly the westward course of the sun, marked by the eastward progress of the splash of sunlight on the lake. He saw that upon the water, cast over and over by the turbulence, innumerable mottled bodies were floating, some already in a state of decay, others just dead. The horrible mud-animals of the cavern depths, attacked by the curse which man had loosed upon himself, were already going the way of all other life. The air was filled with steam, with mingled gases, and with the strange, corrosive compounds produced by combustion. It was hot and stifling, and when one breathed the nose and throat were burned. The old man had a damp cloth over his mouth to protect his lungs from the fiery contact. Nevertheless he clutched repeatedly at his throat, as if with his long talon-fingers he could remove the oppression of the atmosphere.

Nina had resigned herself in stoical fashion to whatever might come. Outwardly she was content and calm. That death would come this week, or next, or this year, or next year could make little difference to herself and her father. Life held no promise for either of them; there was no use to carry it on. Yet in her eyes was betrayed a furious conflict. They were rebellious, though her lips were relaxed and quiet and her slender hands content in her lap.

The old man, lucid for a moment, turned upon his bed. He gazed at her, and reaching out, he took her hand.

"We have lost, my daughter," he said, "and we must be content to follow where the others have shown the way."

"Yes," she answered bitterly.

But a little later she burst out:

"What good is life? On this old Earth our people have lived for a thousand generations. Once they owned and mastered it. Billions of them lived and worked and struggled, survived adversity, planned for their children's children through the ages. Yet it has all come to nothing. It is all ended under the stone, which the sand and salt have covered up. What has the race achieved for its suffering? Death and extinction!"

"No, Nina, no," the other replied. After a little thought, he went on:

"Our physical achievements—they have gone the way of flesh and dreams and all that men have set great store by. But still we cannot say that life was wasted, for every life was worth the living, even though seemingly it came to nothing."

The girl spoke softly, "Our people are dead. With me the race ceases to exist. There will be nothing in all this universe to mark its presence or its passing except the shaft, which may survive the sand. Meanwhile where is your beauty now, your strength, your justification for all the suffering and struggle?"

The old man faltered in his reply. Tears came to his eyes.

"It is an age-old question," he said tenderly. "Nina, with all our science, with all our hard, cold knowledge of the universe, we have never answered that frightful, paramount question: *Whence have we come, and where do we go?* Neither has it been opened to us, the answer to our importunate *"Why?"* In this direction we stand at the end of the world, exactly where we stood at the beginning of it; and those of us who have seen much, and suffered much, and thought much, can only trust in something, as did the cave man in his graven images, the priests in their avenging gods, and the Christians in their Trinity. We can—*we must believe*, Nina—that somewhere there is a compassionate intelligence who rules all things. Either that or we must believe that there is nothing—nothing—"

He turned away wearily, emotion and weakness making him speechless. The flickering pool of sunlight moved steadily eastward across the surface of the lake. The level of the water was going down with alarming rapidity. Steam filled the cavern, almost blotting out the light.

It would soon be night in the world outside, a night that the old man feared would be his last. He shuddered not at the approaching specter of death, but at the dreadful fate in store for Nina. With him gone, she would be left to face the future alone.

The water in the cavern pool could not last more than a few days—a week at most. For eighteen days now the ferment had been at it. For more than three years they had lived in the cavern, sometimes filled with hope, at others times cast into the deepest despair. But always there had seemed a chance that life could be continued until someone would come to the rescue. But one morning Nina had come screaming and incoherent into the tiny cave where they had lived, declaring that the ebony lake had taken fire at last. The Nemesis of the race had sought them out again.

Then they had known it was the end.

"Nina," the old man had said, "we have just time to put our affairs in order, as does a prudent man when he knows Death is at hand. We will tidy our house, so to speak, and go to our eternal rest bravely and with preparation. We must behave as befits the last members of a brave and worthy race."

"But do you think it is too late for rescue? We have a few days yet." Her voice had been quiet, reserved. But the old man shook his head.

"Too late," he said, "only by the merest chance could we be saved now. I think it is better for us not to expect anything. If rescue were coming from the winged creatures which Nino said had taken our message, it would have come sooner."

Nina nodded agreement, reluctantly.

"I suppose so," she said, "but still I have a feeling—that we should hold on a few days.

"Last night it came to me strongly in a dream. It seemed that we were beset by strange animals, which had driven us to a cleft in the rocks and were about to seize us. You had given up the struggle, declaring that all was lost. It seemed that there was no possibility of escape or rescue, for we were cut off on one side by steep walls of rock, and on the other by the beasts attacking us.

"But then, at a time when another moment would have been too late, we heard the whirring of giant wings. Looking upward we beheld men in the air above us. I could not see them distinctly but I felt they were intelligent, able men, fully formed as were any Earthmen, except that they were snowy white. On their backs were fastened broad white wings, which they managed as birds do. They alighted on a rock nearby and drove back the animals and rescued us bodily from imminent death.

"Of course, father, you will say that it was only a silly dream. Yet so vivid was it, that I cannot put the vision out of my memory. There was one whom I have never seen—yet someone, too, whom I seemed to have known for a long time. When the rescuers carried me upward over the cliff this man held me close to him in his powerful arms. I saw that though he seemed of another race, a being literally from another world, there was at the same time something very human about him.

"Today, when I saw the plumes of gas rising from our lake and knew that we were confronted with the end of everything here, it came to me that the dream was not a mere fancy. It was a prophecy. I felt it. I know that we will be rescued!"

There were tears in the old man's eyes when he replied:

"My child," he said, "I wish that I could believe it too. It would be happier so for both of us. But Nina, I am sure that a wish has inspired your dream. Your desire to be saved, coupled no doubt with your youthful, unsatisfied desire for love, is expressed here. In the age when men believed in miracles and prophecy we might have placed faith in this. But science long ago taught us that dreams are never prophetic; that at the most they express to us, often through symbols, the wishes and desires buried in our subconscious selves."

Nina shook her head impatiently.

"I knew you would say that. It is what I have repeatedly tried to tell myself. But father—science may be wrong!"

She had faced him with this declaration so fervently, with such seriousness and intensity, that he looked away hastily. He tried to speak gently, placing his hand upon her arm.

"Nina," he said, "I perceive that you have fallen in love with this curious man-being of whom you have dreamed. I can only say—cherish your dream as you would a reality. It may bring you peace and happiness. We must face the end soon together."

The Last Wish

As well as they could, they placed the meager details of their lives in order as persons might who were under sentence of execution, and knew that there was no reprieve. The old man had gathered his writings and placed them where they could be preserved for anyone in the future who should be interested in inspecting them. The little cave they tidied up for the last time, partly closing it. In that vault they intended their bodies to lay when at last life could be maintained no longer.

Finally the old man asked, "Was the statue broken when Nino's 'bird' sprang the trap?"

Nina shook her head negatively.

"It fell free down the shaft way, as he had planned," she explained. "Its weight carried the ladder up, and in return the increasing weight of the ladder deadened the statue's fall. It is at the bottom now, sound and whole."

The old man appeared to consider this information. "We planned it as an everlasting monument to the figure of mankind," he said. "We wanted it to rest for eternity atop the shaft if we should die here unrescued. It is my desire, Nina, that we respect the race's wish and return it to the top."

The girl breathed rapidly.

"I have been thinking of it, too," she replied at length, "but—I can't do it alone. I have neither hands enough or the necessary strength to raise the statue."

"Then I will help you."

"But you can hardly walk."

"I will not be called upon to walk much more. I will give all my strength, if necessary, in performing this last task."

"Very well," replied the girl. She was plainly reluctant to permit him to sacrifice himself needlessly. "But it will be hard, even with both of us working at it. We lack Nino's knowledge of the mechanical principles of the mechanism."

"Even so, we can do it," said her father impatiently. "Please help me walk through the passage to the tower."

When they had given seven days to the labor of it, the statue was again in place, the trapdoor closed and the tower sealed. The old man, true to his word, had given virtually the last of his strength to the enterprise. Nina had carried him, more than aided him, back to the cavern of the never-ending fire.

There she had laid him on the pallet of herbs beside the diminishing lake, where he could watch the sunlight when it played upon the waters. For herself she had made the little tufted seat nearby where she could sit and look after him.

It was on one such afternoon, when she had been permitting her mind to wander over the grueling labor of the last few days, that she gave a sudden cry of alarm and despair.

"Father," she said, "do you realize that if they should come to rescue us now, we have cut off for them the only avenue by which they might reach us, and the only sign by which they would know that we were still alive!"

The old man turned to stare at her.

"Why?" he asked. "We are still living, and I have not turned off the automatic device which will cause the statue to remain fixed on the tower."

"I know," was the reply. "But we failed to attach the mechanism when we put the statue up. Now it is too late. The locks have taken hold and we are sealed in. No one could enter if they tried, unless they blasted the tower down. And lacking proof that we are still here to be rescued, they would hardly do that."

The old man continued to look at her, without answering.

Beyond him, in the pool, the dancing sunlight was nearing the eastern end of its daily path. Soon it would disappear. Then, without warning, the ground and the interior of the cavern trembled with violence, as if an earthquake had shaken it.

At that moment it seemed as if the end of the world, long in abeyance, had come to extinguish, not only the feeble sparks of life that still remained, but the globed Earth itself. An ominous sound issued forth as a large section of the carved and glowing roof cracked and rumbled overhead. Fire showed at its edges, and then with a mighty splash the great dome broke loose and hurled itself into the boiling depths of the dwindling lake.

The water sputtered. There was a burst of hot steam that filled the cavern. Overhead the fire demons roared and howled. The casque of translucent stone that had confined them had fallen, setting them free.

CHAPTER FIFTEEN
Tellus Again

ALLUS MARCE, with the eighty-nine men of his crew, had brought the new space car safely aground at the edge of the valley, which had once been the bottom of the sea. Like an uncanny demon of brilliant metal, the ship rested on the edge of the sandy desert, which stretched away endlessly, hard and dry and glittering with crystal.

The vast plain was nearly level, except for the depression of the valley. Its carved and gentle surfaces rolled away to the west and north in a series of rounded, sandy hills; and in the blue distance was a chain of mountainous, jagged ridges.

It was the valley that interested Allus Marce and his men, however. They lost no time in going into it. Posting only a small guard, they quickly adjusted themselves to the conditions of weight and atmosphere on Tellus by their gravity nullifying equipment. Then the party moved slowly down to the lowest level of the valley, keeping close together and watching carefully for any sign that might indicate that life still existed.

Straight to the milky shaft at the valley's lowest point they flew. There Allus Marce paused to examine with surprise and delight the statue that he saw had been replaced by human hands since his earlier departure.

"We will now learn," he declared, "whether our trip has been in vain. For when I move this mechanical thumb as it to take away the message it once gripped, it should set in motion the machinery which will open the tower to us."

"But if it does not move?" asked a lieutenant.

"Then," replied Allus Marce, "we will know that it is time for us to return to the suffering moons of Jupiter without the aid we have come so far to seek, and to lead our people all well as we can to their own destiny. It the statue does not move then the race of Tellurians is extinct and we have only wasted time in coming here."

"Then I pray you, Commander, move the thumb!" cried an impatient member of the crew. "This strange, dead world depresses all of us. We are somehow afraid, in this magnificent whiteness. On this Earth there is too much quietness and tragedy."

Allus Marce extended a trembling hand. His fingers grasped the mechanical thumb. At that moment the sad smile of the ebony figure seemed to pierce his very soul. It seemed almost as if the figure were about to speak. He paused a moment nervously, half expecting to hear some sound from the stony lips.

With sudden resolution he moved the thumb aside. He grasped the arm and wrenched it as if he were forcibly removing the cylinder. The thumb snapped back in place. The assembled men from Jupiter drew off a little, awaiting what might happen.

But there was nothing. The figure only bent on them its inscrutable, compassionate smile, its understanding eyes. It did not turn or sigh or plunge through the tower. No trapdoor came to view. And even though they shook it, pried against it, and tried to move it bodily from the sloping roof of the giant milky crystal, they could not make it yield or give them access to the stairway in the tower.

After an hour or so of labor, Allus Marce gave up. "They are gone," he said quietly, with a strange sadness in his voice. "We are too late."

The others prepared to return to the spaceship. Standing upon the edges of the tall monument, which human hands had erected here in the last stronghold of a forgotten race, they seemed like beautiful, eerie birds, poised for flight. They had re-discovered the dead planet, Tellus, and had found it, to their regret, uninhabited and forever uninhabitable. Now they were ready to return.

But in that instant, as Allus Marce stood with his fellows poised for flight to the space car that would bear them home again, he had a strange premonition.

Standing back, he gazed with keen eyes up and down the valley's crumbling walls. His vision caught the deep wound in the aide of the eastern mountain and even as he glanced at it he perceived a tiny wisp, a haze perhaps, lingering over the quarry. For a moment only he stood there, staring at it. Then, spreading his powerful wings, he was off to investigate this phenomenon.

The others followed him. Quickly they moved the jagged rocks aside, exposing the old hole that led into the cavern underneath. Out of it was coming the haze, which attracted Allus Marce's eye. Down inside they could hear, faintly, the roar of the disintegrating waters, the rumble of earthquake and chemical fire, and mingled with all these other sounds certain faint human cries, which caused their hearts to leap.

Allus Marce was the first man through the opening.

The others followed, rushing alter him into the cavern. There they saw in an instant what the shock of the space cars landing had done. Most of the roof of the cavern, with its cold, bubbling fire, had fallen into the puny lake, all but smothering it. Upon the pallet that Nina had made for him, the old man still lay, though life was almost gone. Only in his dimming eyes did consciousness struggle. The remaining fire in the cavern's dome lighted up the scene with lurid brilliance as the clouds of steam and vapor, pouring from the smothered waters, drifted like wraiths through the hot atmosphere.

Nina was kneeling over her father, holding a cup of water to his lips, trying to speak softly and reassuringly, yet distraught herself by the cataclysmic end of the cavern's roof and the burning lake. Her back was toward the opening through which the Jovians had entered. She did not see the approach of her rescuers until she heard the sort syllables of their speech. Turning, she seemed to recognize them, and involuntarily uttered a sharp cry of alarm and hysteria.

Nina and Marce

ALLUS MARCE, glancing at her with admiration, came up and knelt at her feet.

"Perhaps you are—Nina," declared the heir to the House of Allus, remembering the language of the Earth people. "'We are from the planet you call Jupiter. We have come to rescue you."

Nina passed a weary, trembling hand across her eyes. She had a mad moment of delirium, believing that she was again experiencing a dream.

But the old man on the pallet, arousing himself from stupor for a moment, beheld the Jovians also and half arose from his bed, his eyes staring wildly, his long, disheveled hair falling over his withered face.

"Nina—Nina!" he said in a voice both of wonder and alarm. "Do you see them, the winged men you dreamed about?"

"You too?" she cried. The water bowl clattered on the pebbles at her feet. She held her outstretched hands toward Allus Marce, touching him as if to convince herself that he was real. He stood up at her first words.

"Forgive us for welcoming you so crudely," she exclaimed. "We do not know even yet whether we are dreaming. We have been locked in this hole for so long it is small wonder if we have gone a trifle mad."

"Indeed, we are real," replied Allus Marce quietly. "Out-side we have a space car which will carry both of you far from this planet. It is my honor to welcome you to Neina, largest, noblest moon of Jupiter, where you may live with us as persons of the highest rank. Your message, taken from Tellus many months ago, has been received and translated there. We know your history."

"But—we are black, and you are white. Does color make any difference to you?"

"On the contrary. Besides our light will make you white as we are as soon as you have been exposed to it."

"We have nothing with which to repay your kindness."

"We do not ask for pay. Your beauty and gracious presence, and your wisdom in the arts and sciences which we lack in Jupiter and her satellites—these will more than repay us, daughter of Tellus."

Allus Marce saw that the old man was very weak and in immediate need of medical attention. He ordered the physicians of the party to minister to him at once.

"Let us go out into the open air," he said to Nina. "There we can talk with greater ease of Jupiter and the worlds that you shall see."

He perceived that her eyes had consented. Placing his strong arm about her waist, he carried her up through the opening. In a few minutes they were walking on the valley floor, now bathed in shadows.

"My people will be overjoyed at your safety," Allas Marce continued. "For I would have you know that a mighty civil war impends, in which the four satellites seek independence from the oppressions of the rulers on Jupiter. You and your father could aid us in that struggle, in many ways."

"But my father is very old. For weeks I have been expecting his death. I'm afraid he cannot live much longer."

"We have medicines and treatments which will restore him forthwith to health, for he is suffering mostly from exhaustion and exposure. And you, Nina, shall be invested with all the powers of a princess of the land. You shall unite our people to wage common battle against the enemy. You and your father, with your superior knowledge of the science of warfare, shall be of the utmost aid in winning for us our independence."

"I, too, am a lover of peace," he explained gently. "So also are our people, the men of the satellites. But we have been cowardly too long; we have resisted too little, and now we must fight or give up everything. Will you not aid us to independence when slavery is the only alternative?"

"We have seen so much of war," she replied. "We have seen the race of men on Earth engaged in mad contests of self-destruction until death was loosed upon them all. Is it true that there is no peace anywhere in the universe?"

"Struggle and death are the natural accompaniments of life, wherever it is found," the young man explained.

They walked in silence for a short way, and then Allus Marce turned and faced her squarely, taking her shoulders in his strong hands.

"Nina," he said abruptly, "you needed us, and sent a message to us. My people, out of the goodness of their hearts, have raised and financed this expedition to rescue you. We do not ask anything in return for that rescue. We are not here to bargain with you but to offer you life and ease and plenty. But my people also need you. Will you help us?"

"Yes," she said at length. "However we can help you, we will."

Later she stood on the edge of the cliff and stared down into the dry valley that held the crumbling remains of Mansende. "Henceforth," she said, "until a way to restore the Earth is found, the people of the Moons of Jupiter shall be my people, and their needs my needs—if they will accept me as you have accepted me!"

"Then come," said Allus Marce, taking her into his arms and rising straightway toward the entrance to the space car. "Your father is already here and ready, and we are now about to depart. We have no time to lose!"

*   *   *

A little later Nina stood beside Allus Marce at a window of the space car. Below them, already far away, a great yellow disc was spread out in the sky. Upon it in high relief were the dark and ragged patches of land that had once been continents. The seas were still marked by tremendous glittering fields of salt, reflecting the sun's light, even at that distance, with blinding brilliance.

"There," said Nina a little sadly, pointing downward at the disc. "I have lost the Earth!"

Allus Marce held her close to him.

"By that stroke," he replied seriously, "the Moons of Pleida have gained a Queen!"

THE END

Editor's note: Gawain Edwards also wrote a sequel to this novel, "The Return from Jupiter," which Armchair Fiction will be releasing sometime in the near future.